About the

L.G. Kirchgeorg is originally from Switzerland but has spent most of her life in Germany, the US and the UK. She studied English and German in North Carolina at Davidson College (BA) as well as management at the University of Edinburgh Business School (MSc). You can usually find her reading or sipping a gin cocktail while daydreaming about her snowy mountains. *Sex & Summer Wine* is her first novella.

SEX & SUMMER WINE

L.G. Kirchgeorg

SEX & SUMMER WINE

Vanguard Press

VANGUARD PAPERBACK

© Copyright 2021
L.G. Kirchgeorg

A CIP catalogue record for this title is
available from the British Library.

ISBN 978 1 784659 88 2

*Vanguard Press is an imprint of
Pegasus Elliot MacKenzie Publishers Ltd.*
www.pegasuspublishers.com

First Published in 2021

**Vanguard Press
Sheraton House Castle Park
Cambridge England**

Printed & Bound in Great Britain

Dedication

To the girl who dreamt about publishing a book
by the age of twenty-five.

Monza

The First Days of July

The uncomfortable mixture of sweet chinotto and bitter biting bubbles slithered from the tip of my tongue, past the insides of my cheeks and lingered relentlessly in the back of my throat. Campari soda. Even Campari orange would have been better. I closed my eyes, redirected the liquid into my cheeks and forced it down with two strong gulps. Without any conscious effort, I felt my cigarette push its way between my lightly parted lips. I inhaled deeply, shooting the smoke straight into my lungs. Held the toxic breath for a moment. Exhaled. The smoke overpowered the disgusting taste that had accumulated only seconds ago.

A snigger came from across the table, and I opened my eyes to see three bemused silhouettes engulfed in a satin cloud of smoke. I didn't even bother trying to hide my annoyance, redirected my gaze to the half-dead orange roses on the table and took another drag of my cigarette, apparently, the only understanding ally in this group.

We were sitting outside on the terrace of our favourite restaurant despite the pressing heat of the early evening. Silvio's strong, rough and uncomfortably warm hand slid from the back of my chair to the back of my neck. The movement wasn't smooth at all, his hand kept getting stuck on the sweat on my bare back. Yet he didn't recoil at my dampness and took a short drag of his cigarette.

"Sorry, amore." He gently pulled me closer towards him. "I should have remembered that you don't like Campari."

I looked at him and studied the familiar brown threads entangled in his enchantingly green eyes. We held each other's gazes, all that trust we had built over the years suspended between the two of us. Then, I pulled away, redirected my attention to the lifeless cigarette between my fingers and breathed in the hot Monza air that settled uncomfortably on my upper lip.

"Really, Silvio?" began Adamo, tightly holding Elda's hand. "You and Giovanna have been a couple for five years now and you still don't know what aperitif she likes? Even I know it's Aperol spritz."

"Don't even start," I replied monotonously for my boyfriend. I tightened my long black ponytail, which became increasingly sweaty. Even northern Italy couldn't escape the summer heat. I wondered why Elda's white long-sleeved shirt wasn't drowned in sweat. She and Adamo had just come from church and were wearing about twice the amount of clothes than I was. Maybe they were too preoccupied with themselves for the high temperature to crawl into their bubble of joy.

"You know as well as I do that once Silvio is set in

his ways it's as set in stone, as the hieroglyphics in Luxor."

"The what?" asked Adamo vacantly. I shrugged my shoulders and waved him off; explaining would have been more of a bother than it was worth. It was becoming increasingly hard to be the only properly educated one in our group. I hadn't noticed it as much when I was attending business school in Milano. Perhaps I had been too consumed with my studies before to really notice the difference. Yet it had only been a couple of weeks since I had completed my master's degree and I was becoming increasingly aware of the absence of intellect in my friends.

"As long as you know what my favourite drink is, fiancé." Elda smiled as she placed her diamond embellished hand on Adamo's cheek and kissed him tenderly. As if unaware of their location and our presence, the two fused into one like droplets of rain on a smooth surface.

The ring held a small oval cut diamond, which glistened profusely against Elda's heavily tanned hand. I couldn't pull my gaze away from its sparkle... not because I thought the ring was breathtaking, although it was a wonderful selection for the budget that Adamo had. Elda had been delighted she got a ring at all; her father had made so little money that he had proposed to her mother with a fruit bowl, which was supposed to symbolise fruitful happiness. Elda had shown it to me when we were seven years old, and I remember thinking that it didn't so much look like a glorious symbol of love but more like an asymmetrical ceramic plate I could have made in primary school, even though I had the artistic talent of a rock. But I hadn't been able to tear my attention away from the blue bowl, fascinated by its lack of symmetry. And now I couldn't stop gaping at Elda's sparkle either. Except this time not because of its physical appearance but because of what it represented: theoretically, a binding commitment for years to come.

I was truly happy for them because I knew that they could and would make each other content. Five years ago, when Silvio and I had gotten together, Adamo had just been my boyfriend's reserved and stiff best friend and fellow car mechanic. But then I had introduced him to Elda, and this person I thought I had known well just blossomed and grew into a wonderful man who worked beyond his limits to become a new version for his woman.

Adamo embodied a transformation that I only witnessed in the many fictions I had read: defying any manly instinct, Adamo had immediately begun to listen to every single thing Elda had to say and acted on her wishes. He had begun dressing like a potential husband with button down shirts and shaved his jaw spotlessly every single morning. The funny thing about his transformation was that Elda had never demanded it. My best friend's parents' relationship suggested that fruit bowl proposals and romantic frittata dinners were enough. So, Elda's minimalist demands were somewhat inherent. No matter how hard my father had tried to get Elda to choose between cheese and prosciutto, she always ate her bread plain. But still Adamo had experienced the urge to transform into something better for her. Perhaps Adamo had felt compelled to measure up to Elda's impeccable beauty to prove to her that she had made the right selection when she chose from the many suitors she had. She embodied all the values of a good Italian wife: gorgeous, domestic, caring, religious and family-orientated. Adamo probably wanted to ensure that he was worthy of his prized possession.

My man made no such transformation. He hadn't changed in years.

While the freshly betrothed couple became increasingly oblivious of our presence, I placed the cigarette between my lips and checked my phone. Other than the lock screen photo of New York that Mamma had sent a couple of days ago, the display was empty.

I felt Silvio's breath on my cheek and couldn't help but feel comforted by his familiar lips, all dry from the cigarettes and dehydration. He never was very good at staying hydrated, especially in the unbearable heat. His usually wavy blond hair transformed into straight strands that stuck onto his tanned forehead, which made him look like the thirteen-year-old boy I had met in middle school. I hadn't liked him back then, and we lost touch when he had gone to the Istituto Professionale and I had started at the Liceo. But one day, when I had been twenty, Papà's car had broken down and Silvio had been in charge of the repairs.

I pulled my attention away from the empty screen, slowly turned my head towards Silvio, and felt his rough lips stroke my cheek until my smoke-stained mouth met his. With our eyes closed we kissed each other almost shyly; unlike Adamo and Elda, neither one of us liked displaying our emotions for each other in public, especially in that summer when we spent more time destroying our relationship than holding each other's hand. Suddenly conscious of being on full display on one of Monza's busiest piazzas, judgement knocked against the back of my head. I gently but purposefully placed my thumb against his stubbled chin, pushed our faces apart and replaced my mouth with my cigarette to fill his searching lips. Silvio opened his eyes with hesitant surprise, sat back upright as he clamped the cigarette between his ring and middle finger, not bothering to inhale.

"So Silvio, when will you finally propose to Giovanna?" Elda asked and I could feel my organs turn into concrete as I forced myself to look innocently at the joyful couple.

I opened my mouth, but thankfully Silvio was faster because I would have just expressed phrases of anxiety. "Elda, I'm sure you know that the two of you will be the first to know when the time comes," he said and placed my cigarette between his lips, this time taking an actual deep inhale. I felt completely useless without my weightless drug between my fingers.

"Yes, yes, I know," she said easily with her typical sweet smile plastered on her face, "Adamo told me that you have talked about it, though."

She wasn't lying. Silvio and I had talked about it a few months before. Before I had graduated, before I had started my rough and tiring job as a barista, before I had given up hope that I would get a real job that actually justified my seemingly endless years of education.

And before I had started sleeping with another man.

But that was just a temporary thing, completely separate from my long-term relationship. That man could never love me like Silvio would.

***

Silvio's familiar weight collapsed on top of me. He tried to steady his breathing and buried his face in the nape of my neck, his stubbly cheek tickling my skin. I wrapped one arm around his muscular back and stroked his hair with the other. Lying like this was comfortable, so familiar. I could not recall feeling safer than when I was lying in his arms, his toned body pressed against mine. Five years later the sex was still undeniably good. We liked our little experiments.

The sun had just set. We laid there for a little until the rising and falling of his strong chest became even. He pushed himself up with one arm, and his golden cross dangled back and forth around his neck. He looked down at me with tenderness and love.

His blond hair fell into his eyes, and I gently brushed it away with my fingers. In that moment, he looked so much like the twenty-year-old boy I had fallen for as soon as I had stepped foot into the car dealership to pick up Papà. When Silvio had caught sight of me in the doorway, his youthful face recognised me instantly. After he had reintroduced himself and smiled the childlike grin that hadn't vanished since I had last seen him in middle school, I finally remembered who he was. Then, Silvio had done something no other man who found me attractive had ever been capable of: he had stretched out his strong arm to shake my hand. I had hesitated for a second, at first not understanding what he was trying to achieve. Eventually I had realised that some men were capable of politeness and respect. I had taken his hand, felt his rough and broken but undeniably comforting warm skin against mine, and I had known intuitively that this young man would be different.

Papà, a highly-educated man, hadn't approved at first, but once he had recognised Silvio's care for me, he accepted the relationship. Silvio and I had fallen in love so quickly and so deeply, I had never questioned whether we were right for each other. Why should I have done? We had been twenty, naïve and he treated me like a goddess, like the deity that every woman secretly wanted to be seen as.

Back then I had been convinced that that's all a woman needed, a man who made her his own personal idol. Even when I had accidentally insulted the church in front of his extremely religious mother, Silvio had sided with me even though he cherished her. It had been the biggest fight he ever had with her and took two weeks to resolve. She had wanted him to find a more suitable woman, someone who cherished the church, but he had insisted that he would rather rebel against his family than leave me. The blow of this statement had been as much of a shock to me as it was to his mother.

"Water?" he asked, pulling me out of my nostalgia. Without a response he got up, which allowed me to study his impressive backside. Silvio was truly a beautiful man.

I knew that objectively I was not bad to look at. But most Italian men were probably more attracted to my enchanting exoticism rather than anything else. My genes were so kind as to give me the best of both worlds — Mamma's olive skin, her thick black hair, her flat but delicate nose. But I looked more Italian than Chinese; my eyes were huge and my body very curvy compared to Mamma's. My cheek bones and my deep golden tan I got from Papà. I was the definition of the mixture that Italian men found attractive. That didn't mean that they treated me right, especially when I had started university. But then Silvio had become the biggest part of my life, and all those undeletable, emotional and physical memories had been replaced with his unconditional love.

Silvio returned with two glasses of water and

slipped back under the sheets. He passed me a glass, and I took a big gulp. The uncomfortable cold slithered through my sweaty body, and I placed the water on the bed stand. Reaching for my cigarettes, I passed him one, lightly plucked another out of the box and placed it between my lips. I reached for my lighter, but Silvio was quicker and already held the dancing light in front of my face. When the flame kissed the cigarette, I could already feel my satisfied body go limp with relaxation even though I hadn't inhaled yet.

As we smoked, he reached out his hand and placed it on my naked waist, making me withdraw as fast as a rabbit in danger. "Your hand is freezing," I said, with a much more accusing voice than I intended.

"Sorry, amore," he said with a chuckle and relaxed into his pillow, cigarette in one hand and the glass of water in the other. I studied the golden cross on his chest. I never really understood why he wore it. His mother was Roman Catholic and his father would join his wife at church but Silvio barely ever went to any services.

In my family, books and education were our source of guidance. Works like *The Odyssey* and *The Tempest* constituted my bible. The closest my family ever got to any sort of spiritual engagement was when we acknowledged the architecture of a church. Our lack of the Roman Catholic practice was always a point of conflict between Silvio's parents and me. Having a gay mother who had left her family to pursue a career while the father had to look after the child was not exactly a daily occurrence in Monza. Education and career were really not of great value in Silvio's family. And yet I tried and tried to get Silvio interested in my intellectual passions. The academic gap between us had given me a superiority, and it made me increasingly question the viability of our relationship.

"Did you finally get around to reading my master's thesis?" I asked, although I already knew the answer. Silvio never much cared for my paper on the comparison between the developmental policies of Italy and China. He wasn't stupid, he could understand if he really tried and would listen to my explanations. If he tried to understand politics as much as he understood every single bolt and screw of a car, he could honestly work for the United Nations.

"For your poli — and... analysis—"

"Yes, yes, for my politics and policy analysis degree, you know this," I said impatiently, with my cigarette between my dry lips. As if someone slapped me hard across the face, I felt anger quell impatiently in my chest and covered my nakedness with the blanket.

"No, amore, I haven't," he said nonchalantly. "You know I probably wouldn't understand a word anyway."

"Stop it, stop selling yourself short," I shot back angrily, "You haven't even tried. You know I can help you understand."

Silvio scrambled out of bed muttering and threw the half-smoked cigarette into the ashtray without extinguishing it. He banged the glass of water on the bedside and put on his black boxer shorts and T-shirt, letting his toned abs vanish from sight.

"Silvio," I said almost pleadingly, as he made to leave the room. He stopped in his tracks to look at me. "Please don't always walk away when we talk about this."

"What is so important about the fact that you have some wise old guy's book on some crisis on your bedside table and I have a car magazine on mine?" he asked, throwing his right hand into the air as he sat down next to me on the bed. "We love each other, right? That's the only thing that is important, Giovanna."

"Sure, but I want to make sure that our conversations go beyond just asking about each other's day and where we should go for our vacation. You always want to go to Rimini, Silvio, there is nothing to plan!"

"Fine, you choose where we should go."

Silvio was back on his feet again. I too got up, clasped the cigarette between my lips, grabbed the orange dress I had worn earlier and threw it on, not bothering with a bra or my underpants. In the process of throwing on my clothing, I accidentally chucked the cigarette to the floor. Without thinking, I extinguished it with my bare foot and felt my skin burn, but I didn't care, fury seemed to consume the pain. Unconsciously I stemmed my arms against my hips like his mother would and gave Silvio the most reproachful look I could muster. Inhaling sharply, I wiped the sweat off my forehead and tried to calm down.

"This is not about Rimini," I said, as calmly as possible. "I need you to at least think about the things I care about. When I ask you to read the article, it is because it's important to me." I couldn't stop the crescendo in my voice. "When I ask you to read what I spent months writing, I expect you to read it."

"But it's just not interesting to me." Silvio's mouth was shaped in a dangerously thin line.

"And you think that your stories about that one car that had a specific type of screw loose, which you fixed is interesting to me?" I took a step forward and our heaving chests touched. "No! But I know it is important to you, so I listen."

His green eyes glistened dangerously and at first, I thought he was going to pull my hair and throw me to the ground. Instead, he shot his hand against the nape of my neck, grabbed my waist with the other and kissed me so forcefully that a squeal escaped somewhere in the back of my dry throat. My arms were trapped against his chest and were pressing painfully against my breasts. With all my strength I pushed him away and he loosened his grip. His eyes were angry but also full of love and desire. We stood there for a couple of seconds, then I grabbed a prize-winning non-fiction book Papà had given me from my bedside table and flung it into my bag.

"Where are you going?" he asked with such

tenderness in his voice, I was startled by how quickly he could transform.

"I'm going home. I'm sleeping at Papà's," I said, not meeting his eyes, fully conscious that I would not be sleeping at Papà's but at another man's.

"That's what we do, Giovanna," he began gently holding my arm in his. "We fight, we kiss and love each other."

Taking a deep breath, I heard myself whisper: "I don't know if that's enough any more." I pulled out of his gentle grip and paced out of the door.

***

The typical mixture of pasta, fresh flowers and smoke of Papà's apartment filled me with such instant comfort, I might as well have been a little girl again. I had just spent the night in Milano with the other man and didn't want to see Silvio just yet; I was still so utterly frustrated with my boyfriend. If he at least tried to invest some time into my passions, I would have known that he appreciated what I was capable of, other than being a girlfriend.

I hadn't been home for a while and felt instantly secure and settled. Papà didn't hear me come in, and I watched him water his lavender plants that were silently resting in the living room. He looked down tenderly on the little lilac strands, just like Nonna did before she died. The cigarette dangled lifelessly between his bearded lips, probably forgotten as soon as he turned his attention to his joyful flowers; the tiny spark of fire was eating all the paper away like a grasshopper that feeds on a leaf. Some ash fell onto the rustic carpet.

Mamma had left so many years ago, I had barely been at an age where I read books over fifty pages, but Papà was lonelier this summer than straight after she had departed for America; he spent most of his time at the school, teaching and working on his lesson plans, but there was only so much planning that a teacher at the liceo could do. Papà was a traditionalist but had been oddly supportive of Mamma when she had realised she liked women as much as Papà did. Yet he had still held onto her and continued to love her like no change had occurred. That was, until she had decided to move away. Somehow, he had seen past his anger and pain when Mamma needed a fresh start in New York. And when New York University had offered her a position as an economics professor, he had to let her go. I was still working on that. I knew she wanted to protect me; she had considered taking me with her but at that point I hadn't spoken a word of English and both my parents had also agreed that Manhattan was not the best place for a seven-year-old to grow up. And Mamma had needed her space to sort out her new identity. She had never said it out loud but I think she really didn't want me around while she was trying to figure out who she was; I would have been a distraction.

"You'd better put that cigarette out or you'll burn

yourself," I smiled at him, when he spotted me in the doorway.

"Giovanna," he said, with his loud and comforting voice, as he placed the watering can on the floor, got rid of the cigarette and walked over with open arms like an eagle in mid-flight.

"Ciao, Papà," I choked as I hugged my father.

Before I could even think of the source for my stifled voice, I felt a tear run down my cheek and held Papà even more tightly, his steel glasses pressing against my ear. He was the parent who had raised me, the one who had grounded me for coming home drunk when I was sixteen, the one who had dried so many heartbroken tears from the age of fourteen before Silvio became my companion. I really missed Mamma; the one phone call every other week could only carry a relationship between a mother and a daughter to a certain extent. As soon as she had stepped on the plane to New York, Mamma had become a mentor to me. She was never the mother I needed. I expected a parent to stay with a child.

"Giogio." He spoke into my tangled hair that must have fallen into his face. "What's wrong?" Though he tried, he couldn't hide the note of surprise and concern, which triggered another tear to spill out of my eye.

I opened my mouth and closed it silently. What *was* wrong? Perhaps these were tears of guilt for sleeping with another man over the past six weeks? No, I told myself naïvely; that was a completely separate story.

"Come, Giogio." He loosened our embrace and led me to the sofa. I sat down, avoiding my father's eyes, and studied the chipped purple nail polish on my long fingers. He sat down in the seat across from the sofa, and I sensed him studying me. I felt guilty for worrying him. I might as well have been twenty-two again when he had found the pregnancy test at the bottom of the bathroom trash just days before I had moved out to live with Silvio. The test had been negative, but I had never seen Papà's face engraved with so much disappointment and fear. Of course, he wanted to be a nonno someday, but he wanted me to pursue my degrees and work in politics first. Clearly the latter of the two was not going according to plan unless you wanted to call pouring coffee for the occasional male customer dressed in a suit a political career.

My tears had dried. We just sat there silently as a jumble of words raced to the tip of my tongue. Yet I was not able to compose a sentence that could articulate what I was feeling. My conscience didn't know, so how could some spoken words? I let the silence speak for me.

Papà sighed and eventually said quite bluntly, "Well, this must either be about work or Silvio, or both."

The dusty beige sunset tickled Papà from the side and illuminated the fingerprints and dust that had collected on his glasses. I told him he should clean them, but he ignored my comment and looked at me expectantly. I couldn't dodge him any longer. "You know the barista thing is tiresome, otherwise work is all right."

"Well, you can still take the summer tutoring job I got you, you know?" he sighed, a little exacerbated.

"I already told you that now I'm done with my studies I want to stand on my own two feet." I attempted to keep the annoyance out of my voice. "As much as you have done for me and as much as I love you, Papà, I have to learn that I can't always have you help me find my way."

"That's fine, Giovanna. And yet the only reason you are a barista is because Caffè Bianco hired you right away. That job was always supposed to be a short-term solution. I think it's wonderful that you read all that nonfiction on politics and volunteer, but you might as well sit on the couch and eat chocolate all day if you're hoping this will get you a job. So, where else have you applied in the past two weeks?"

I forced myself to keep eye contact with Papà, though I felt my crossed legs tense up and curled my hands into fists. "I haven't…" I broke off, took a deep breath and said a little more forcefully than I usually dared, "When you apply to twenty positions and they either offer you an internship or a rejection, it is hard to sustain any sort of faith that anyone would truly want me."

"Then you'll have to apply to another twenty and see what happens." Papà's comforting tone turned into his authoritarian teacher voice I had never learned not to fear. "You're more than qualified, and I don't want to see you throw away the sixteen years of education just because you didn't spread your talented wings wide enough." He rubbed his forehead with his hand, and his thick, grey hair slid into his face. He looked so old, in that moment, I couldn't help but think that his worrying escalated his ageing. He sighed and continued, "Twenty applications are not enough with the current job market, Giovanna. Success will not fall into your lap in the world out there. The job market is no classroom. Nowadays it takes relentless patience and ambition to get anywhere, not laziness."

Something sharp punctured my chest; being called lazy and without ambition by Papà hurt. "Look." I spoke as clearly as possible, not believing that I had cried in his arms just a moment ago. "I'm a grownup and I'm fine with being a barista. Stop sounding like—" I caught myself just in time before I almost blurted out the name of the man, I was having an affair with. I quickly ended the sentence with, "Stop sounding like Mamma."

"So, you have talked to her about this then?"

"She called me last week." I shrugged. "She says it's fine to be in transition. The job will come along eventually."

Papà's sad eyes broke away from my gaze and he pulled out a cigarette from his lined shirt pocket. It almost touched his lips. He hesitated. Still not meeting my eyes, he passed the cigarette to me and took a second one out for himself.

"The job won't come along, Giovanna. It has to be found."

Papà opened his mouth, and I waited for him to talk about the different ways I should apply myself to the world. But his preaching never came. He touched the tip of the cigarette with his antique silver lighter, got up and sat next to me on the sofa. He held out his silently glowing cigarette. A peace offering. I placed my cigarette against his and breathed in until I felt the smoke fill my lungs.

The fatherly affection had returned in his brown eyes, completely devoid of any overbearing authority. He reached out his hand and patted my cheek three times like he always did. It was my turn to say something.

"Papà?"

"Giogio?"

"I know you didn't approve of Silvio at the very beginning because he didn't go to the liceo, yet alone to university—"

"There is a tacit wisdom within that man," Papà interrupted kindly, so I took another drag of my cigarette, then placed it on the ashtray. "No education could have ever given him that."

"That's right," I agreed sincerely, and turned to the question I had been thinking about ever since I had graduated. "But you *do* think that Silvio is right for me, yes?"

My father studied me. His thoughts, oddly illegible. "I never met a man who cherished his woman more than Silvio does. He has his faults, he is set in his ways, but that young man really loves you."

"That's a yes then?" I asked, not quite knowing what response I really wanted to hear.

"If what you seek from a man is unconditional adoration, then yes."

"So, love is enough to be happy?"

Papà placed his arm lightly around my shoulders and looked at me with the unstoppable sadness lingering in the wrinkles around his eyes. "It certainly wasn't enough for your mother. I gave her all the love I could collect, but she still decided to fall in love with a woman. For some people love can be restricting if they want to grow and transform."

"But love would have been enough for you?" I asked quietly, again not knowing what answer I was expecting or hoping to hear.

"Yes, for me it would have been enough."

***

The apartment was empty even though it was dinner time. Silvio had agreed to cook for me, but he was still drinking with Adamo or perhaps with his parents, I wasn't sure. I didn't really listen to his plans after we had made up; my head had been buzzing with Silvio's words of kindness and tenderness. His forgiveness was overwhelming, and though I was used to his words of affection, this time there was something pleading and desperate in his voice. It made the electricity between us peculiarly distorted. Undeniably pleasant, yes, I loved feeling desired, but also strained. I wasn't quite sure what to do with this new dynamic that increasingly crawled its way into the midst of our relationship.

Silvio had said he would try harder to fulfil my expectations. he had whispered that he would cook for me tonight as he nuzzled my neck after my shower. When he set his mind to something, he had this remarkable ability to stubbornly see it through. Two years ago, Adamo had bet Silvio that he wouldn't be able to run a marathon in half a year. But my man hadn't only proven all of us wrong, he ran the thing four months after the bet was made. He had loved his new passion to such great extent that he had even started a sport physiology course. He had completed the certificate with excellent grades, I was still so proud of him. When it came to his manhood, Silvio knew how to impress the world. He was actually training again for a marathon in October.

And yet his ambition was a pure technicality; despite his promise, he had already let me down. Could he really only prove himself when it came to demonstrating the traditional definition of manhood? How terribly patriarchal.

Pasta with his mother's homemade pesto, it really wasn't anything complicated to cook. But apparently, it was already too hard to remember that he was supposed to show up on time in the first place.

Even though his words of promise had been spoken only this afternoon, I was more concerned about the numbness in my chest. I was expecting anger to draw through my veins as if sucking up burning liquid through a plastic straw. Instead, emptiness engulfed my heart, leaving the pumping organ numb and abandoned.

My black leather loafers flew across the living room like cannon balls as I flicked my legs as hard as possible to get rid of them. I was mistaken, there was an unconscious animation within me after all.

Silvio and I had just talked a few hours ago, right?

I quickly strode across the living room, my bare feet squeaking sharply against the cold fake wooden floor. The walk barely took three seconds because of the tiny apartment we were renting. It wasn't like Silvio could afford a bigger one, and I wasn't really making money at Bianco.

The bedsheets were still rumpled lumps that looked like twirled icebergs. He had spoken all of these wonderful things that I wanted to believe, no, *needed* to believe, amongst those misshaped sculptures. I destroyed the shapes right away as soon as I entered the bedroom. I clenched one of the blue blankets in my fists and froze, debating whether I should be throwing the bedding out of the window, or exercising my duty as the woman in the relationship and making the bed. I let the blanket slither between my olive hands and paced into the kitchen.

A mess of dirty dishes and a suspicious smell of decaying vegetables swamped me, which made me take a step back. Our kitchen had not been in such a catastrophic condition this morning, but the immense summer heat of the day accelerated the need to bring out the trash. Furiously but somehow without tearing it, I flung the trash bag out of its basket, pulled on the plastic strips to knot them together and threw the wretched thing into the hallway. Not waiting to see whether the stinking mess landed against Signor Rossini's door, I slammed the apartment door shut.

Clearly there was an abundant angry burning flooding through my core. Good, it meant that I hadn't completely given up on Silvio.

Cigarettes and wine. I was in desperate need of cigarettes and wine.

My feet annoyingly indecisive, I tumbled left and right as I let my body figure out what I craved first: my cigarettes, which were lying in the bedroom to my left, or wine, which stood in the pathetically messy kitchen to my right. Avoiding the smell, my body gravitated to my cigarettes.

With angrily shaking hands I managed to let the flame suck gently on the paper. I inhaled sharply, let the lighter fall and pulled the cigarette out of my mouth. There was no denying that I was a pro at smoking, but in my anger, I managed to swallow too much smoke, which was now tearing on the lining in my lungs. I coughed several times and dragged the cigarette back between my lips as I tried to recover — I really needed the nicotine. Though the burning subsided, the manic tickling in the back of my throat did not. I could feel my legs hurry into the reeking kitchen as I ripped open the Pinot Grigio that we had been drinking two days ago. Not bothering with a glass, I allowed the liquid to still the relentlessly scratching itch and felt disgusted with myself despite the wonderful comfort; I could not believe I was drinking white wine out of the bottle. This situation with Silvio was driving me into outrageous behaviours.

Violently grabbing the bottle out of my mouth, I replaced it, with my cigarette and poured a more than generous amount of the yellow-green liquid into a wine glass to somehow redeem myself from my crass behaviour.

Giovanna, breathe.

And I took a breath. Without the smell of wine under my nose or the cigarette sucking on my dry lips. I simply breathed in the sweltering Italian summer air, forcing my mind to clear into a vacuum.

So much anger. So much feeling just because he forgot to make me pasta. For a split-second I wondered where it all came from, but I knew. There was a limit to how much of Silvio's inert character I could take. Exercising my intellectualism with my books or Papà could only satisfy me so much. I wanted to talk about the financial crisis, climate change, the conflicts in the

Middle East, the refugee crisis, with the man I loved. Even Silvio's perfect words from this morning could not soften the line between love and utter frustration.

My empty lips longed for some sort of touch, and I found myself holding both my white wine and the cigarette, which was slowly dying between my fingers. I studied the burning orange glow as I let myself take a comforting sip of Pinot Grigio. The pleasantly cold liquid gently caressed the insides of my mouth before I swallowed the alcohol.

I took both my source of nicotine and liquid salvation in my hands, walked into the pitiful excuse one could call a living room, and relaxed myself into the yellow, fake, leather sofa, which squeaked and squirmed as I released my weight into its softness.

I allowed myself to breathe and recover as I alternated between cigarette and wine, between nicotine and alcohol, between bad habit and numbness.

The Last Days of July

"Where were you?" Silvio stood in the door frame, his beautiful face engraved with worry.

I was with another man, I thought to myself, but quickly slapped myself in the face with common sense. "I had a late shift at Bianco, then went for a walk in the park and got lost in my book." I looked down my black loafers trying to hide the guilt and didn't want to give him any indication that I had too much alcohol. "Sorry, Silvio, I should have called."

I walked into the living room and gazed at the silent clock on the wall. It was two in the morning; no wonder Silvio's green eyes were strained with worry. There was no way he believed my excuse. My feet swiveled to face him, and I did my best to hide my intoxication. He deserved so much better. I locked my eyes with his and felt the guilt quell in my chest, all the way into the senseless edges of my ears. He walked over to me, took my head between his hands and gently tilted my face, which forced me to look straight at him.

"Do you have anything to tell me, Giovanna?" he asked and I was too drunk to discern whether his question accompanied genuine suspicion. Probably the latter, Silvio had a good instinct for people, it was basically a sixth sense. Once, we had made a picnic in the park to enjoy some fresh air and he had been the one who pointed out that a young man had looked extremely anxious next to his girlfriend. And indeed, the boyfriend had broken it off with her only minutes later; we had watched a loud slap strike the man's cheek, followed by uncontrollable sobs by the woman. Silvio and I had been quite affected by this spectacle. He had put an arm around my shoulders and pulled me so close like magnets who couldn't help but cling to each other, as if to assure me that he would never hurt me like that.

I tilted my head into his right hand, closed my eyes in exhaustion and then opened them again. "No, amore," I replied.

"I know your mother taught you to bottle up your feelings, but you know you can tell me everything, right?"

I nodded into his hands, fully aware that I had never abided by Mamma's life lessons; she wasn't exactly the pinnacle of a good Chinese woman either, so whenever she had imparted her traditional wisdom, I had always just nodded along. She could be such a hypocrite.

Silvio wrapped his arms around me. I reciprocated the gesture gratefully. How could I have ever cheated on Silvio? Repeatedly! My companion, my love. It must have been his expression of concern that helped me sober up. My hand touched his cheek, and I let my thumb explore his lightly bearded skin, even though I knew every inch of its surface so dearly. He leaned his head into my sweaty hand and closed his eyes.

Guilt. So much guilt. No woman would ever measure up to his incomparable dedication.

Silvio wanted to have sex. But I had just had sex. And too much wine.

Exhaustion spread through my body like a deathly cancer. My body fell limply into Silvio's muscular arms, and he carried me to our bed, just like a baby. It amazed me how much I loved him. The alcohol climbed into every fold of my brain, into my thoughts and experiences.

For an hour, I passed out. A complete mess. In the arms of Silvio. And still, I was a deity to him. His tolerance for my rash actions was unconditional. Even after I had gotten utterly wasted after my graduation and thrown up all over him while he was asleep in bed, he had shown no sign of disgust; all that had mattered to him was that I was fine. He had changed the sheets, slipped my clothes off and had taken me into the shower to clean me up. He had even given me a passionate kiss despite the taste of vomit that had lingered in my mouth.

Sometime before dawn, my eyes flew open with a racing heart. He was asleep, his arms tightly wrapped around me. My vision was still spinning, and I felt the sweat and seemingly inescapable heat stick to my skin. I pushed Silvio away from me. He opened his eyes in relaxed surprise; I must have pushed him away much more forcefully than I intended because he woke up to my strength, which was saying something because the muscles that clung to me were merely a formality.

I felt Silvio's head rest itself against my chest, his strong muscular leg pushing itself under my skinny one, and I suppressed a sigh. He didn't understand I was boiling with heat.

"Remember when we went to Rimini for the first time, and we were naked in the ocean?" He spoke into my covered chest. I had trouble understanding him as he mumbled into me but nodded in agreement and through habit placed my tired hands onto his blond hair. His waves looked all grey in the pale moonlight, which shone into our small bedroom. I used to imagine what he would look like when he was old and had actual grey hair, but the thought became increasingly hard to puzzle together.

He chuckled into my blanket. "That's when I knew I truly loved you."

I opened my eyes and looked down, expecting to find him thirstily gazing at me. Instead, I found him to be just as tired as I was, his head still comfortably resting against my chest.

"We hadn't even been dating for six weeks. We were twenty, Silvio," I whispered hoarsely and cleared my throat to get rid of the phlegm that had accumulated from the combination of alcohol, tiredness and smoke.

Silvio stayed silent for a little, which almost made me fall asleep again until his voice cut through our tiredness: "I know, but I knew you were the woman for me, Giovanna. To this day, I haven't understood how a simple guy like me could end up with an amazing woman like you..."

Inhaling, which raised my chest, I had the right words ready: how accomplished and wise he was, how I never understood why I ended up with such a wonderful man, how impressed I was with his marathon training, how he understood cars beyond the simple mechanics just like he did with people. But as I dragged for the breath to say these words, I also knew that these accomplishments were not enough any more. Now that I was sleeping with a man who in many ways was so beyond Silvio's capabilities, I couldn't say these words out loud. I felt guilty enough as it was. During my daydreams, they were no longer Silvio's words that rang in my brain, but the words of the man who told me to get rid of my boyfriend to fulfil the potential that I hypothetically represented.

Instead, I exhaled. "I am glad you feel this lucky." I let go of his hair, gently pushed his heavy head aside and turned to face away from him.

The First Weekend of August

That weekend in August, an unbearable heatwave roamed the alleys of Italy, which prompted one of our rare weekend trips to the country. When Silvio had announced that his uncle's family was on holiday, which meant that the charming little house at the Lago di Como was empty, I had given him a soft sensual kiss on the lips, feeling my spirits rise. A weekend away from the sticky and trapped heat was exactly what our relationship needed. The past couple of weeks had been full of heated arguments with him, which also meant a lot more make-up sex than I would have bargained for.

Then, Silvio had announced that Adamo and Elda were coming too. I had felt the flame of excitement suffocate under a bubble of annoyance. I treasured Adamo, and Elda was truly my best friend. She had been the one who helped me fix my hair after I had tried to cut my own bangs. He had been the one who taught me how to prepare the best tiramisu in all of northern Italy. But the reality was that I wouldn't have chosen their companionship if I met them today. It was painful to admit, but I had truly outgrown them because of my education. It was enough work to come to terms with Silvio but to spend the whole weekend with my boyfriend *and* the newly engaged couple was testing my patience.

The one hour drive to Como was quite an experience. I could feel the memory carve itself into the back of my brain. Adamo's car was an old Alfa Romeo from the eighties, which was in an oddly fragile state despite the fact that a car mechanic owned the white vehicle. To make matters worse, as soon as we pushed our way through Monza's Friday afternoon traffic with the heat pressing down on the car like a heavy pile of books, the air conditioning broke. Despite the heat, Adamo decided to keep the sickening and dirty highway air out of our lungs, even though I weakly protested; we were all smoking in the car anyway, so I really didn't see a big difference. The satin clouds of smoke were dense and grey, but the discomfort of the heat was so penetrating that we didn't feel the need to interrupt our unhealthy habit. I sucked the life out of the cigarette, which now rested uselessly between my fingers. I opened the window. A violent gust of heated air pollution slapped me in the face and roared angrily into my left ear. I threw out the cigarette butt as fast I could and fumbled for the window button to keep the vicious turmoil out of the car.

Silvio, who was sitting in the back with me amongst the abundance of Elda's luggage — she never knew how to travel light — leaned into the gap between the two front seats and started tinkering with seemingly random buttons while Adamo swore loudly. Elda turned up the music to extinguish her fiancé's curses.

The heat gnawed at me like a chew toy and the disgusting sweat pressing its way out of my skin came as a pleasant guest; it did indeed cool my body ever so slightly. The usually loose dark green top that I was wearing stuck so firmly to my skin, it almost looked like it had become part of my body.

The heat had consumed so much of my energy, I merely registered what Silvio was mumbling under his breath. Elda and Adamo had fallen silent, probably trying to concentrate on anything but the heat. I let my head fall limply against the warm window. The vibration of the old car was anything but pleasant against my pounding head, but the cooler temperature relieved some of the pain.

"There," exclaimed Silvio only a few minutes later. The icy air blasted its way onto my damp skin from all these different angles. I had been feeling so miserable and annoyed this whole trip so far, I did not think my boyfriend would be capable of fixing the air conditioning. But he did. He didn't win so many customers at work without reason. The dealership hadn't been doing well. Then, Silvio had come along with a skilled hand and heart, whereafter the business had started booming. His boss had actually nicknamed him 'Gamechanger'. I had always thought that was some strange insider joke amongst mechanics. But it was meant literally. Silvio was great at what he did. A violent hand squeezed my heart. Guilt. Perhaps I had never given Silvio enough credit for his accomplishments. Correction. I knew that I had never given him enough credit for his accomplishments.

Silvio sat back down on his seat and fastened his seat belt. His dark grey T-shirt was stained almost black with sweat because he had been simultaneously crouching and standing in a tiny car that trapped heat like a sauna.

"Marvellous," Adamo told his friend. "I'm glad I'm behind the wheel. There was no way I could have fixed the thing so quickly, if at all."

"Oh fiancé, you're good at what you do," said Elda, as she stroked Adamo's sweaty cheek and leaned towards the air conditioning, allowing the strong blast of wind to hit her right in the face. Her short wavy hair flung and twirled around her head like the snakes of Medusa. It made her dark brown waves look longer than usual.

"It's all relative," sighed Adamo as he kissed Elda's hand. "I'll make a better husband than a mechanic, I can tell you that for sure."

Silvio giggled so youthfully, he reminded me of the innocent orphaned kids I read to a few times a month. There was still something so boyish about my love, I couldn't help but feel enchanted by him. When our gazes met, I realised that I was beaming at him full of true admiration, and he presented me with a smile. He leaned towards me, right arm outstretched, and gently whisked my flying black strands of hair out of my face.

I studied the little pearls of water on his nose and tried to remember what he used to look like without his stubble framing his face.

By the time we got to the little house on the lake, we all looked as if we had conquered a massive hurricane. The satin smoke that was trapped in our car had faded, and the cold had definitely dried parts of our clothes but we were all visibly exhausted. Getting out of the vehicle, I felt the settling crunching sound of the pebble stones beneath my white trainers and took a step away from the car. Air. Still hot, but fresh.

The small lake house looked exactly as I remembered: the thick white stone walls, the wooden frames, the big windows that invited the sunlight into the house and the wild garden that sheltered the small building like a sea shell protecting its pearl. The sight of tranquillity and the fact that everything was still the same made the edges of my mouth twitch. I was exhausted, but being away from Monza and Milano made the car ride feel like an easy price to pay.

A damp hand tapped my shoulder and Adamo's glistening face greeted me as I turned. He gestured me to help unload the car with Silvio. Elda had already gone inside without grabbing a single bag. The traditionalist believed that biology pre-determined men to carry out the heavy lifting. Meanwhile, my considerate boyfriend had my black weekend bag wrapped around his strong shoulder. My gaze was fixed on his muscular legs that were more prominent than usual; he had run twelve kilometres earlier that morning.

I took one of Elda's shabby old leather bags and was startled by its heaviness, despite its medium size. Curiously, I unzipped the bag and caught a glimpse of colourful sunscreen bottles, shampoo, countless make-up products (the cheap kind) and some other containers. I had no idea what use they had. A chuckle caught itself in the back of my throat. Clearly, she had never heard of travel-sized toiletries.

The cool air that the walls of the house conserved kissed every inch of my sweaty skin. I threw off my shoes almost desperately and enjoyed the satisfying cold stone vibrate through me as my bare skin touched the smooth ground. I took a deep breath and smelled the familiar mixture of cold stone and tender wood mingling within my nose.

Adamo came in with the remaining luggage from the car, and I walked into one of the bedrooms to make space for him in the narrow and dark corridor. My man was on the small double bed, eyes closed. He didn't hear me come in. I quietly tiptoed around to his side of the bed and pulled out my water bottle, which was resting at the top of my tote bag. Though I made a lot of noise as I pulled out and unscrewed the lid of the warm bottle, Silvio still didn't seem to have noticed my presence.

And I struck.

As soon as the first droplet hit Silvio's already damp face, his eyes flung open in alarm. Giggling, I poured the water all over him. He tried to move away, but then his surprise transformed into playful revenge. Instead of retreating, he jumped from the bed and tried to rip the water bottle out of my hand, but I managed to empty it in the last moment. I laughed as I watched his playfully disappointed face, and he looked down at the empty bottle as if it were a foreign object.

Then his lips formed his boyish and mischievous half-smile, which made my laughter stop right away. "You're in a lot of trouble, amore," he took a step towards me, shaking his head.

Slowly, as if I were an impala carefully retreating from a hungry cheetah, I stepped backwards, not breaking eye contact. Then, I bolted and ran out of the room. It probably took less than fifteen seconds and Silvio caught up with me, pulled me roughly by the arm, lunged me into his chest and somehow threw me into his arms. Carrying me like a baby, he made his way out of the house.

As the humid air pushed down on us, I frantically wiggled my legs and produced sounds that were something between giggles and screams, it must have looked like something from a romantic comedy. I knew what was coming, but before I could even begin to request whether he could take my clothes off, I felt the exhilarating plunging sensation as Silvio jumped off the wooden jetty and into the Lago di Como.

The water was icy cold against my flushed skin, and I felt Silvio's grip loosen as I gasped for air just to find myself swallowing earthy water. Still underwater,

I began to cough and felt my legs automatically cut their way against the water. My head ripped through the surface. I gasped for breath and felt a shock of air shoot into the back of my lungs. Thereafter, I returned to coughing while I trod water. Silvio's arms creeped from behind, and he tried to steady me as I got my breathing under control. He pulled me towards him and I felt his sturdy chest press against my back. He held me above the water surface.

"I've got you," he whispered into my ear and the coughing had stopped. I let him hold me for a little while longer, then I turned to face him. His wavy blond hair was plastered to his forehead. As always, my hand automatically pushed it out of his face. His arms pulled me closer towards him. I wrapped my legs around his torso while he treaded water to prevent us from sinking. This was my personal brand of safety, this moment, wrapped around his body, knowing that he would keep both of us afloat.

"I love you, Silvio." He smiled at me but there was a sadness lingering behind the green of his eyes. I kissed him softly on the mouth to get rid of the strange melancholy that quietly wrapped itself around him. It worked a little bit.

I asked him what was wrong, and he tentatively answered that it had been a while since he heard me say those words. He wasn't wrong. It wasn't a conscious decision but I hadn't said those words to him in a very long time. I had always kidded myself that sleeping with another man would not affect the way I truly felt about Silvio because my boyfriend formed my other life, the simple life that I adored. But clearly, I had been very naïve. I knew that I had just been lying to myself. And to the man I loved.

As if he could hear what I was thinking, he asked, "You wouldn't lie to me, Giovanna, right?"

"I wouldn't lie to you," I tilted my head and was slightly anxious but my voice was remarkably steady and neutral. Obviously, that wasn't an excuse, but technically I wasn't even lying but omitting certain pieces of information. "I really do love you, never forget that." I held his head between my wet hands and repressed a cold shudder that slithered down my spine and into the tips of my toes. He leaned his head against mine, and I closed my eyes.

Safe.

Our weekend together was not the burden I had thought it would be; it was everything I'd wished for. Spending time with Adamo and Elda was filled with lots of laughter and cheap wine, while my alone time with Silvio made me feel like I was twenty years old again: easily excitable, giggly and capable of a kind of love I didn't know was hidden within my every nerve.

As shallow as it sounds, the days by the lake embodied the perfect simple life. It had been a while since I last imagined that this version of myself could make me feel completely content. This weekend away from Monza and Milano stopped the screaming voice inside my head that I wanted more out of my life than weekends by the lake, holidays in Rimini and a wholesome family. This weekend made me believe that Silvio would be more than enough.

I didn't have to be the person who goes out and seizes opportunities like Mamma did when she had moved to New York. I didn't need the fancy wine and apartment. I didn't have to become part of the Italian political constitution like my dad believed I could. I didn't have to be the version of myself that the man I was having the affair with said I could be. I didn't need all of these things.

It was Sunday when the heat wave broke. It was still hot because it was August and it was Italy, but the temperature that morning felt like a warm embrace rather than a wet catastrophe that drenched you as soon as you set foot outside of the house. Adamo and Elda were still sleeping off the Pinot Grigio from the night before, so Silvio and I decided to enjoy the beautiful summer morning after we had spent a passionate hour in bed.

As we stepped outside the house, I felt the wonderful cold catch itself in my hair, which was soaked wet from the shower I had taken only minutes before. The pleasant air twirled around my bare legs and played with the bottom of my yellow summer wrap dress, which made my skin glow brown instead of olive. Silvio came up from behind me and was buttoning his white shirt, which made his toned torso vanish from sight. My man looked so handsome and attractive. I had forgotten what effect a proper shirt had on him. If he stood next to the CEO right now, it would have been hard to tell, which one the more successful one was; Silvio could dress the part, no question.

He led me away from the house and took my hand. We were both barefoot. I felt my skin soak up the pleasant chill of the shade from the weeping willows as we walked silently away from the house and enjoyed the endless land, which his uncle owned. The birds twittered so enthusiastically, I couldn't decide whether it blended in with this scene of nature or whether it was just purely annoying. I decided to go with the former and allowed the sweet whistles to blend into the scene. The grass was still damp and I felt the undersides of my feet take in the vitality of the grass, which was damp from the night.

Tranquillity at its finest.

I felt Silvio's grip loosen around my hand, and I turned to look at his beautiful face. His lightly calloused hand let go of mine. He smiled at me nervously. There was something tense around his mouth and a worry constricted his usually lively eyes.

Contradicting his usual romantic nature, he didn't get down on one knee. But I knew this man so well that I recognised what was coming before a single syllable escaped his mouth. My throat constricted. My eyes felt wetter than usual, and I lost all sense of my body. I read about these sensations in the romantic novels I rarely picked up, and I never thought that any of these clichés were actually going to hold true. And here I was feeling everything that all these fictional characters represented. Complete and paralysed shock.

Though was I really shocked? I always figured that this day would come unless I decided to breakup with Silvio beforehand. Which I hadn't. I loved him, I adored the way he worshipped me, the way no other man ever would. And I knew that this should have been enough. Silvio offered protection, safety and an adoration no one else could ever measure up to.

The choice seemed so simple. Why wouldn't I choose the man who could offer me unconditional love? Why wouldn't I choose the man who cherished every single perk and nerve that I embodied? Truly, the choice seemed so simple.

Silvio's lips were moving and I could read exactly what they were saying, but I couldn't hear a single word; the birds seemed to have left their nests and flown straight into my ears. All I could hear was their annoyingly loud twittering.

A growing pain swelled uncomfortably within my chest. I thought I'd had a heart attack, until I realised I'd stopped breathing. It was painful. Perhaps quitting smoking was a good idea after all.

The ring glistened seductively even in the shade of the trees. Silvio had told me about his grandmother's ring, the wonderfully big square-cut diamond with two sapphires on either side, one of his family's prized possessions. I had imagined its gloriousness, had imagined it placed on my ring finger when Silvio told me about it several years ago, but my imagination was far from reality. The diamond was so big and majestic, I had to consciously allow myself to breathe.

I looked into the hopeful eyes of the wonderful man who wanted to marry me. I wondered what my face looked like. Was I smiling? Was I crying? Was my face carved in stone?

My ears could no longer discern the songs of the birds that were whistling through the trees. A ringing was all my ears could acknowledge.

Milano

That Day in June

The jug full of delicious cold milk was poured all the way to the brim. Naturally, I spilled the fresh whiteness onto the stone floor. With a splash, the milk formed a sloppy half-moon shape sprinkled with little white stars around its core. I quickly scanned Caffè Bianco in embarrassment. Empty. I always thought it was a cliché that the highly educated made for terrible baristas but there was a lot more truth to it than I would have ever admitted out loud. Two weeks here and I still had trouble operating the coffee machines. I took a deep breath and enjoyed the strange mixture of the cold caffè air and the summer heat whirling inside my nostrils. I pulled my long black hair behind my ears, flicked the damp white cloth off my shoulder and knelt on the wonderfully cold stone to get rid of the imperfect half-moon spillage.

"One cappuccino, signora," he said.

I hadn't heard him come into Bianco. Just by the sound of his low voice I knew I would be attracted to him. The sounds that escaped this man's lips promised charisma, seduction and an unpredictable harshness. Pushing myself up from the mess I made, I stood before the man. A clean-shaven smile greeted my slightly unkempt appearance. I smiled back and glanced at the time. Eleven o'clock. I used to frown upon Italians who would order a cappuccino past ten o'clock in the morning but his penetrating gaze piercing through his soft blue eyes dismissed my principles right away.

"It's, signorina, actually," I replied, blushing at my bold response as I turned to press the right buttons.

As I prepared the cappuccino, I could not help but sneak secretive glances at the man, although it must have been blatantly obvious to any onlooker that I was fascinated by him. At that point, I couldn't put my finger down on why. He wore a perfectly fitted dark grey suit, but I had these sorts of customers come in all the time, the ones that were from around Monza and commuted into Milano. I wasn't exactly attracted to his presentation of himself although a man in a dark suit and a clean white shirt was indisputably attractive. I was impressed by his strong jaw, which was remarkably clean-shaven, considering the thick brown hair that framed his round and kind face.

Our gazes met and I could finally pinpoint the softness around his eyes; he was rounder in the face and around his middle, but only a little. It was refreshing. Then, I recognised who he was. He had spoken at the Bocconi Business School about his innovation technology start-up just a week before my master's graduation. *The Economist* had just done a profile on the man as one of the most successful Europeans to break through the noise of start-up businesses. Marcello

Lombardi. That was his name. It was strange to see him here in Monza. He was born and bred in Milano, so it almost felt as if this suburb was oddly shabby for such an accomplished man.

"There you go," I said quietly as I concentrated on not spilling the hot cappuccino all over the counter.

"When are you leaving this place?" he asked, and I must have stared at him in complete bewilderment because he added, "There is something about you that tells me that your job as a barista is not what you are supposed to be doing."

"That's right, it's just a temporary gig." I shrugged and pretended to type something into the computer.

He nodded and I could feel his eyes studying me as he took out three euros from his wallet. I hadn't felt an attraction when he had stood at the podium at Bocconi, perhaps he had been too far away then. But in that moment with only a counter between us I had never felt so seduced by a man. It was strange. All he did was order a cappuccino. I couldn't help but tear myself from the screen to meet the seductive glistening in his eyes. Our gazes locked, and to this day I couldn't tell you why. While I was utterly attracted to the man, his look searched for something beyond desire.

Then one of our regulars entered the caffè, and I forced myself to break away from his intimidating, yet exhilarating stare. "Ciao, Giovanna," shouted Signora Belotti, with her grandchild jumping up and down like an excited parrot. Distractedly, I waved at the elderly lady and returned to focus on the man who took a couple of steps away from the counter.

"Una buona giornata, Signorina," he said.

I nodded. Then he left.

A week later I was sleeping with him.

The First Days of July

I leaned my head against the cold window of the train and instinctively watched the flickering strands of light from the houses of Milano. Strange. It was almost midnight on a Thursday, and yet there were still so many glows. Half closing my eyes, the strands of light became a hazy overexposed moving photograph that lost its focus the closer you looked at the picture. A complete haze. That was the difference between Monza and Milano, the difference between a suburb and a metropolitan city, between the predictable and unpredictable lifestyle.

I forced my vision away from the dancing strands of light and peered at my own reflection in the window. The harsh train light coming from above made my cheek bones look so prominent, as if I had contoured that feature with a dark grey make-up pallet. The mascara I had been wearing all day on my straight but long lashes was quietly flaking off. Instinctively my thumb gently stroked the bottom of my left eye, then my index finger took care of the right. Otherwise, I wasn't wearing any makeup and looked tired or may have simply felt less energised without it. I wasn't even wearing perfume. The scent of my sweet, flowery and expensive Dior perfume — one of my very few splurges — always made me feel a little more complete.

I never intended to go home and see Papà because I knew he would worry. He would have asked why Silvio and I were fighting again, how the job search was going, whether I had talked to Mamma recently… All the answers to these questions were not what he would have hoped to hear. No, I didn't want to worry Papà. I would spend the weekend with him once I found my composure and made amends with Silvio.

Marcello had surprised me when he said I should come over. It had been my intention to go and see him but I had not been able to get a single grammatically correct sentence out when I called him. I had just assumed he would tell me to go to bed and call in the morning when I was my "usual" collected self. It was the first time he had witnessed my loss of composure even though we had been seeing and sleeping with each other for a few weeks. Most men scared easily. Marcello was not one of them.

As I got off the train, cigarette loosely dangling between my lips, the sticky city summer air engulfed me in a comforting cloud of warmth. The platform of Milano Centrale was busy, and I made my way to the exit. It was midnight, the time where it was wonderfully bearable to leave the indoors in the hot summer months. I inhaled deeply when the single flame of the lighter sucked on the edge of the cigarette.

The architecture of the station was impressive even

in the darkness, perhaps even more so than in the daytime. The shadows that the streetlamps conjured made the solitary pigeons dawdling on the stone look like giants and the columns of the building appeared much wider and deeper than in the daylight. I walked on the street that brought me closer to the man I had longed to see ever since I had left his apartment three days before.

The way to his place felt longer than usual because the groups of people at the train station began to scatter into the different streets of the city. There was no one around to distract me from the distance between Marcello and me, other than the occasional homeless person sleeping in the side alleys I passed. A pang of guilt quietly combusted in my throat; it had been a while since I last did any form of volunteering. I couldn't believe how much I had neglected it. For several years, I had been heavily active in fundraisers and had worked with several homeless shelters to look into different ways that the living conditions there could be improved. I had been so passionate about these projects and took the lead in several organisations. This kind of leadership had been so valuable to me, it really gave me a purpose. This feeling of helping strangers had been so rewarding, it was the reason why I wanted to go into politics. But here I was, too busy thinking about myself. Feeling lost and uncertain about the future apparently did that to you.

I paced past the blurry shapes of shabby Alfa

Romeos, some solid Volkswagens, but also a Maserati, a Ferrari and Tesla. Usually, I took my time to admire fast sports cars, secretly liked the idea of owning one someday despite my terrible driving skills, but I was so focused on getting to the man that these luxuries blended with all the ordinary cars. In that moment, they were all worthless to me.

I finally arrived outside his building and buzzed his apartment. I heard the high-pitched ring that allowed me to enter only a moment after I touched the brass button. He was efficient even when it came to opening a door.

Stepping into the cold marble lobby, I couldn't help but shiver; the contrast of the summer warmth and the cold that radiated from the stones was striking. I quickly made my way to the elevator and pressed the button to the top floor.

The elevator quietly ascended upwards, and I felt heat flood from my chest all the way down to my toes as I looked at myself in the mirror. My appearance was so much worse than the train window had let on; my eyes had lost their vivacity even with the remains of mascara, my usual slick hair was dishevelled from sex with Silvio and my orange dress looked as if I had been wearing it for the past four days. It was also then that I noticed that I wasn't wearing any underwear, hadn't shaved my legs since the last time I had been here and reeked of cigarettes. Marcello didn't smoke, and he had never said that the odour bothered him, but what non-smoker liked the smell of cigarettes?

I lunged across the elevator, hectically pressed random buttons, but it was too late. The elevator doors opened like a curtain at the theatre. I could discern a thin stream of light that stemmed from his door standing ajar before the motion detector triggered the uncomfortably bright light in the corridor.

Though my brain was screaming not to, I let my feet carry me towards his door and walked into his apartment with as much confidence and femininity as I could muster. The whiteness of his opulent apartment was almost brighter than the lights that slapped me when I walked out of the elevator. The corridor seemed shorter compared to the last time Marcello and I had walked through it together almost statically, our hands touching but not holding onto each other. Now, I felt an invisible hand push me down the endless whiteness as I frantically rubbed the mascara off from below my eyes, the thin skin burning in anger. I passed the mirror of his apartment and purposefully gazed at the empty wall on the other side, avoiding the reality of my dishevelled exterior.

His long and elegant black sofa was empty and his fireplace silent and clean like it had never been used before. I walked towards the kitchen to find it just as silent and took a few steps towards his bedroom, but then stopped myself from opening the door; I had no right to barge into his room just because I was sleeping with him. So, I settled myself onto the uncomfortably modern couch in the living room.

I must have been craving the scent of perfume that I had forgotten to put on because I could smell the mixture of fresh lavender and manly wood before I saw him come out of his bedroom. His blue eyes locked with mine, then he studied my ruffled hair and the creased dress. Self-consciously, I almost followed his gaze but decided to glance at the strange expressionistic blue-green painting that represented some sort of emotion, or so he claimed. The blue streaks were entangled with astoundingly endless shades of thick green, which all accumulated at the bottom right corner to create an even shade of turquoise.

"I am glad you called," his gentle voice interrupted my pretend-study of the painting I wished to understand as something more than just a delicate jumble of colours.

"Really?" I couldn't hide the surprise in my voice as I turned to face his kind and round face. Though he nodded I went on rambling, "I shouldn't have called, I apologise for my incoherence earlier, I was a little flustered, I shouldn't have called."

"As I said, I am glad you called," Marcello looked at my face quite bemusedly. I tried to direct my consciousness into preventing the redness in my cheeks from spreading all over my face. He walked towards me, and I just stood there rooted to the spot. I could hear him inhale as my smoke-stained smell crawled into his nose, but he didn't say anything. His soft hand touched my bare shoulder and he gave me a tender kiss on the cheek. I felt my body tense, the self-consciousness stronger than his lovely gesture. He noticed my discomfort too and playfully shook my shoulder with a smile, which made me relax a little.

"Can I take a shower?" I asked shyly, and he nodded.

It was almost as if the hot water sprinkled new life onto me, washing off all the self-consciousness I had experienced as I stepped into his apartment. With a large grey towel wrapped around me, I looked into the mirror and the clouds of steam that twirled around my head and shoulders entertained me for a couple of seconds until my skin adapted to the room temperature. The cheap make-up, which flaked off over the course of the day, had vanished. Only a few remains of mascara were entangled in my wet lashes. It was strange because usually I felt uncomfortable not wearing makeup in front of a man I was trying to impress, but the hot water flushed my face in a flattering and revitalising way. I felt strangely confident, indeed, I felt thrillingly bold. I decided against wearing my shabby orange dress, walked into the wardrobe in Marcello's bedroom and flung on one of his Zegna shirts instead. The pale blue button-down created a mini-dress for me, just like in the movies. I had always wanted to do that, a teenage fantasy fulfilled. The smell of dry-cleaning mingled with my steamy odour.

As I walked into the living room, I tied my long black hair into a knot with the hair tie I had around my wrist. Marcello had his thick-framed brown glasses on and was sitting on the sofa, looking relaxed in his white polo shirt and dark blue trousers. He didn't hear me come in, his attention fixed on the newspaper he was reading, and I couldn't help but smile at this intellectual sight. There he was, an accomplished man in glasses, dressed in a polo shirt and reading a newspaper. Marcello was very tech-savvy, so it was surprising to see him read a real physical paper.

Not wanting to disturb his concentration, I walked over to the couch and sat down next to him, the squeaking of the leather against my naked legs announcing my presence. He didn't pull his focus away from the paper, but gave a small smile to acknowledge my company. Folding the rustling paper in half, he placed the news on the glass table and pulled his right leg up onto the sofa, casually angling himself to face me.

"Feel refreshed?" he asked as he reached for a glass of sparkling water from the living room table that he must have prepared earlier and handed it to me. Taking a large gulp of water, I nodded. I let the pleasantly metallic bubbles burst against my tongue and cheeks. "You look beautiful," he added simply, not commenting on the shirt or anything else. Marcello was a minimalist when it came to language.

A warm glow radiated from within my chest, and I felt the heat pleasantly bloom into my cheeks. I pulled my legs up onto the sofa, careful not to reveal the fact that I was still not wearing underwear. Then, I realised that my legs weren't perfectly shaven and tried to place them back to the ground, but all of a sudden Marcello's hand grabbed my left foot and studied my heel. Worriedly, he placed his thumb on my foot. It took me a while to realise what he was doing. Though I didn't feel the pain, I realised that he must have found the burn mark on my foot, which I had gotten only hours before when I furiously extinguished the cigarette with my bare skin during the argument with Silvio.

Mumbling something about stepping on a stone, I slowly pulled my foot out of Marcello's grip and slid it back on the ground. As if he could see through me, a quizzical look framed his face, it made me feel transparent. I directed my attention back to my sparkling water, placed it on the glass table and then locked eyes with him again. There was tiredness entangled within his quizzical look. I wondered whether it was because he was exhausted from work or whether he was annoyed with me. The silence was growing and made me increasingly uncomfortable, so I had to choose between discomfort, which I hated more than anything, or audible communication.

"We just had a small argument earlier, that's all," I forced myself to maintain eye contact, even when annoyance pierced through his pupils. In my head, I defended myself and Silvio, but decided against speaking the words out loud; it would have sounded pathetic and completely unconvincing.

"But he is still worth it, yes?" asked Marcello neutrally, the annoyance that pierced through only seconds ago vanishing so quickly, I wondered whether I had misread it before.

I sighed through my nod. "I don't want to discuss him with you. You are completely separate from my life in Monza."

"He's holding you back." He ignored me and took off his glasses, which made his eyes look smaller. "I wouldn't even ask if he didn't stunt the potential that you have."

"How could he? He doesn't even know what I want to do."

"Do *you* know what you want to do?" he asked reproachfully.

I got to my feet, took a couple of steps away from him, but then just stood there like an idiot rooted to the spot; this wasn't my apartment, there was nowhere I could really go other than leave, which I didn't want to do. I stemmed my arms against my hips. "No, I don't know what I really want to do, other than work in politics."

"So, is this boyfriend of yours helping you figure out how to get there?"

The silence that followed was answer enough. He too got up, walked towards me and placed his soft hands on either side of my shoulders. His face was full or urgency but also kindness. Still, I couldn't help but feel belittled.

"Look, Giovanna," he leaned his head against my forehead, and I was startled by the affectionate gesture. This wasn't Marcello's style. "I just want you to succeed. And I don't think that your boyfriend really understands and supports you in that process. You're an undoubtedly amazing woman."

He kissed me tenderly, and I let myself enjoy the clean taste of his mouth, which wasn't corrupted with years of cigarette smoke. Even though I was annoyed with him mentoring me, I felt myself enjoy his warm and soft body pressed against mine and wrapped my arms around his strong back, pulling him closer. His hand rested reassuringly against the nape of my neck and his tenderness turned into passion, but not in a sexual way. I searched for the explanation of the urgency under his polo shirt, tried to find the answers within his mouth, but I couldn't.

It was the first time we saw each other and didn't end up having sex. It was late, although this had never held us back before. We just fell asleep next to each other. No cuddling, no words of seduction, just sleep.

***

Sweet, gentle, bitter, pleasant burn. I let the red wine stroke every cheek wall, let it spread all over my tongue, felt it rush between my teeth. My eyes were closed to experience its abundant flavour. A very playful wine. Though I was accustomed to the usual cheap and the occasional mediocre wine on special occasions, the elegant taste of this expensive liquid was undeniable. Marcello had good taste even though he didn't drink any more, yet for some unexplained reason he owned an enormous wine cellar, which was hiding behind a secret door, disguised as a bookshelf.

"What do you think about this Tuscan Lodovico wine? Do you smell the difference here in the Antinori Tenuta di Biserno?" He nudged my glass towards me. A little puzzled I leaned down, my long hair falling onto the table, and smelled the accumulation of red. The strong scent of wood and berry twirled inside my nostrils just like it did with the glass I had drunk half an hour ago. I could barely taste the difference — there was no way I would *smell* something that differed. Obviously, there must have been a discernible difference between the two of them, but I was not well-versed in wines, so the fancy bottles of elegance all just tasted expensive to me.

As a response, I simply nodded as confidently as I could. Marcello's round face tilted a little to his left and the sides of his mouth twitched. Busted. Though I still had a lot of trouble understanding the man of few words, there were little gestures that he used repeatedly where I just knew what they meant. The massaging of his index finger meant that he was deep in thought, and I learned not to ask or interrupt this pensive experience. Raised eyebrows indicated not so much surprise, as I usually read the little movement, but concern. And the twitching of the sides of his mouth was my least favourite as I saw it as his recognition of my lack of intellectualism, the feeling of belittlement flushing my skin every time.

He took a sip of his water and looked down his empty plate. I followed his gaze and studied the juice of the steak remains, the brown and bloody stains clinging to the white plate. The graceful twirls of spinach covered the rest of the unclean whiteness. Marcello didn't order any carbs. Perhaps he was trying to lose some weight, though I was obviously not bold and stupid enough to ask. A couple of days before, when I had asked him why he didn't drink alcohol, he had shrugged, simply told me how he had stopped three years ago after his marriage ended, and got up to get something, which I had been glad about because it was the first time, I'd heard he had been married. My face must have had looked like he'd punched me in the stomach.

"Did you enjoy the dinner?" I asked almost shyly, and I wished I had a more confident note in my voice. Clearly, I was intimidated by the man, but he didn't repeatedly have to know about my admiration for him.

"I did," he said and smiled at me. "Shall we get the bill and go back to my place?"

"Yes, I think that would be nice," I reciprocated the smile.

"Does your mother enjoy teaching at NYU?" he asked out of the blue.

Quite taken aback, I gave him a quizzical look. Though I had told him about her living in New York, I had never given him any indication that she was a topic I really wanted to discuss. For me, her abandonment was still a subject of disappointment and confusion, so my strategy of ignoring her actions had carried me through all these years. I didn't feel the need to reconcile my feelings about Mamma with Marcello.

"I think so, I haven't called her in a while." I folded the napkin from my lap to avoid looking at him.

"The US education system is so different. Does she prefer it?"

Clearly, he didn't get the hint that Mamma wasn't a possible discussion. "Probably, the high school system there makes more sense than in Italy," I began responding to my napkin but then faced him. "Can we not talk about her?"

"All right," he replied with a strong finality in his voice, indicating that he respected my request. It was quite interesting because Marcello knew how to push the limits when he talked about Silvio but he cut me some slack when it came to Mamma. Interesting.

We sat in silence for a little, our eyes directed away from each other. I wasn't angry at him for asking, but I noticed that he thought he had crossed a line. I wasn't sure if he looked a tiny bit unsettled or whether I read too much into his pensive gaze.

Then, all of a sudden, his vacant facial expression turned into instant animation. "I would like you to come with me to the start-up conference in Genoa next weekend."

Thankful that I wasn't sipping my wine as he said those words — I would have probably snorted into the expensive liquid — I tried to look composed. It was a mystery to me how the subject of my mother had anything to do with a conference. I was glad about the change of topic but with Marcello it was often a game of jumping from one extreme to the next. An unpredictable man.

In a peculiarly low voice I asked, "What is the conference about?"

"The future of start-up businesses in terms of digitalisation and the monopolisation of the industry." his usual soft expression hardened into his business face. It was remarkable how just the thought of work transformed Marcello into such a fierce business man.

"That sounds very interesting indeed, considering the recent theory that the number of successful start-up businesses is going down." I tried not to sound too smug. I had subscribed to *The Economist* two weeks ago, even though I had no physical money to pay for it. However, I needed this sort of investment if I wanted to feel that I was somewhat clever enough to be with Marcello.

"So, you are coming with me?"

Right, I hadn't answered the question and the weight of the subject had only really just started to dawn on me. Of course, I wanted to go with him. It meant he wasn't ashamed of being with a much younger and directionless woman, which was a thought that was increasingly pressing against the back of my mind. It also meant that we would be seen together in an official capacity. I would look like the gold-digger I knew I was not. I was with Marcello because I was attracted to his mixture of humanity and accomplished success. But the people at the conference wouldn't see that from the outside. If I were to see a young woman who could still be in her late teens with a middle-aged CEO, my conclusion would jump straight to the sugar daddy phenomenon, no question.

"Yes," I heard myself say, before I could truly evaluate my feelings towards being perceived as the gold-digging trophy wife. Then, my boyfriend crossed my mind. What on earth was I going to tell Silvio?

Marcello nodded satisfactorily, then waved for the check, which came less than two minutes later. The air of authority surrounding him was undeniable, even when he wasn't running his tech company. He took his brown horn glasses out of their leather case and fiddled for his black wallet to pay for our expensive night. The first night he had spent so much money on me, I felt quite uncomfortable. The bill had been high. I should have had offered to pay my half but it felt oddly inadequate, so I just thanked him. Besides, I had no money to cover this sort of bill.

Though I tried to shove him out of my mind, Silvio's boyish face kept pushing its way back into my conscious. I wasn't a great liar. I had pulled a fib at some point or the other but it never contained hurtful information. Sometimes Papà had asked whether I did well on my Italo Calvino essay, and I claimed I did though I had failed miserably. Yet I had never lied when I knew that the information could be extremely hurtful. I couldn't even imagine the pain Silvio would experience if he knew about Marcello. Silvio... my love... What the fuck was I doing?

On the car ride home, Marcello and I barely spoke a word to each other. It wasn't even that he had to concentrate on the streets; his driver, Signor Lorenzo, chauffeured us through the city. While he looked relaxed and studied the lights of Milano, I studied the ruffled rim of my tight black dress. It had belonged to Mamma. Apparently, she had worn it all the time on the dates with Papà before she was pregnant with me. Though I thought of Silvio the whole ride home, it helped that I was wearing a dress that belonged to a cheater. When Mamma had still been married and questioned her sexuality, she started seeing this woman she had met at her pottery class. The affair had been short and educational. Papà and I had never met the woman. She had just been Mamma's trial period, no one of great significance.

I knew that Mamma cheating on her husband was different; she had been figuring out whether she liked women and didn't want to risk losing Papà in case she changed her mind. On the other hand, she had been lost too. And if there was one thing that had defined me ever since I graduated it was just that: feeling lost. Though clearly this didn't give me an excuse to cheat on the man I loved. But in that moment, wearing the dress of a cheater, I felt it was a little more justified. Maybe. Maybe not.

I really craved a cigarette. The last time I'd had one was in the early afternoon and I cursed myself now for not indulging in one right before I went to meet Marcello. Perfume and toothpaste were there for a reason, I could have easily covered up the smell. My hands were longing to feel its weightless body pressed between my index and ring finger, the desire was quite ridiculous. Instinctively, I almost pushed my hand under my nose to try and smell the nicotine stains but quickly suppressed the urge, aware that Marcello could be watching.

As we entered the apartment and took off our shoes, he placed his warm hand on my lower back and led me straight to his bedroom. We stopped outside the room, and he gave me a gentle kiss on the cheek, his perfectly shaven skin caressing mine as he leaned in. It was such a sweet and benevolent gesture, I was a little taken aback; from what I had been able to tell so far, Marcello wasn't prone to displaying physical affection outside of the bedroom.

"Are you OK?" he whispered, as his hand stroked the side of my arm. His blue eyes settled soothingly on mine, and I couldn't help but feel an utter longing for him. He had a quality that made me forget everything I had left behind in Monza, which made the act of cheating seem less of a sin. His soft gaze and anticipation expelled the guilt, and I nodded in response.

He opened the white door and led me into his bedroom. The subtle scent of his fresh cologne and expensive dry-cleaned shirts greeted me. I walked towards the window and looked down on the pebbled street, deserted of any human movement. It was almost midnight. Several lights were still on in the building on the opposite side. If you squinted, the scattered lights almost looked like yellow stars resting in a cloudless sky.

Marcello closed the door behind him, which always struck me as weird. It wasn't like anyone would walk in on us. Ever since I had found out that he had been married, I had started speculating whether they had separate bedrooms, but that was probably a far-fetched guess. Maybe the insistence on closing doors was just part of the proper etiquette.

Though I didn't turn to face him, I heard him walk up behind me, his soft but strong body pushing carefully against my back. His hands rested on my shoulders, and I leaned against his chest, our bodies warming each other in the chilly apartment. We stayed like this for a while, just leaning against each other, his head resting against the side of my head, watching the lights of the street.

Then, without moving the rest of his body to sustain

the comfort we gave each other, his hand wandered away from my shoulder searching for my zipper. As he opened my dress, my body felt freed from its constricting fabric and I enjoyed the relaxing sensation that pulsated around my chest and hips as soon as Marcello got to the bottom of the zipper. With his chest still against my back, he helped me out of the dress and started kissing my bare shoulders. I closed my eyes, the Milanese starry alley vanishing from sight, and enjoyed his soft lips exploring my skin. Then I turned to face him, and we began kissing each other. Gently at first.

I unbuttoned his white shirt, pushed it off his shoulders, pulled his hot torso towards mine, while he unhooked my bra skilfully and lost himself in my long hair. He tasted so clean, felt urgent and soft all at the same time. A very different man than what I had been used to. The sort of man I hadn't known I would ever crave.

His arms wrapped tightly around my vulnerable nakedness, his hands clinging to my skin. I found his belt, which made a loud clinking noise as the steel buckle fell to the floor. Our lips pulled away from each other. I watched him study my young body, his gaze lingering on my full breasts. I unbuttoned his trousers and pulled them down in one smooth tug, surprised by my own skill. Usually, I wasn't very graceful when I undressed a man.

My hands found his dark hair and took in the subtle waves that hid below their seemingly straight appearance. Our eyes met. Moment of hesitation. I pulled his hips closer, his desire growing the more I pressed against him. He began kissing the side of my neck, exhaling into my flushed skin.

He led us to his perfectly made bed.

Then, the bodies of a young lost woman and an unbelievably successful man fused into one.

The Last Days of July

The nerves I experienced leading up to the conference were much stronger than when I had taken my final examinations. I wanted to believe that I was an adequate match for Marcello beyond looking pretty and performing satisfying moves in the bedroom. I wanted to be good enough, no, *had* to be good enough for him. After all of these years of studying, didn't I deserve to be the right person for him? I knew I was good enough for Silvio, that had never been a question. But I had to prove to myself that I was capable of measuring up to the air of success that surrounded Marcello. The more time I spent with my affair, the higher the ambition became to embody the version of myself that Marcello believed I could be.

I had lied to Silvio that I would spend the weekend at Papà's because of the solitary summer he was experiencing. Silvio hadn't even looked at me, but just nodded distractedly as he was cutting the onions for dinner. He had stared at the onions like they were his enemy, so I pushed him out of the way rather forcefully and continued the simple task of cutting the vegetable into smaller pieces. Though I had been annoyed with him for fussing over such a simple domestic task, I apologised. That had been the least I could have done, considering that I was going to spend the weekend away with another man.

Marcello had organised Signor Lorenzo for the journey to Genoa. It had been then that I realised that either Marcello didn't own a car or didn't enjoy driving. Perhaps he didn't even know how to drive. This was another one of these personal questions I felt I wouldn't get a very truthful answer to. The night after he had invited me to the conference, we had been lying in bed after some excellent sex, his sweaty body clinging to mine, and I had gathered the courage to ask him about his parents. He had answered that they were still alive and lived in Bari, then started kissing me. But I had pressed the matter and asked what his relationship with them was like, hoping that he was relaxed enough to share a little bit of his past. Of course, he hadn't let anything slip, and had just answered that he had never been close with his parents but 'they were there'. When it came to personal questions, he never gave me much to work with. It was very frustrating.

We spent most of the car ride in silence. He worked on some notes, and I read *The Economist* even though I really craved the contemporary fiction novel that was silently resting in my tote bag. I didn't have the guts to pull it out and read it in front of him; it wasn't the kind of intellectualism he would find worthy. His giant bookshelf in the living room only consisted of non-fiction such as biographies, business handbooks and literature on history, not a single fiction book in sight. So, the assumption that he wouldn't approve of my book seemed only logical to me. I was also too shy to ask to stop by a gas station because I really had to use the bathroom and the traffic turned the two-hour journey into a three-hour one. Evidently, Marcello was in deep thought; not only was he massaging his index finger more vigorously than usual, but he also never asked Signor Lorenzo to stop at a gas station. My bladder was bursting from all the coffee I had drunk before the trip, but I was really too much of a chicken to ask for a break. Therefore, I distracted myself with my nerves about the conference, the relentless fluttering of insects in my stomach becoming wilder the closer we got to Genoa. God, I just wanted a cigarette. But I had decided not to give into my cravings while Marcello was present.

Out of the blue, Marcello's voice pulled me out of my preoccupation. "Are you excited, Giovanna?"

I looked at him and his kind smile settled me a little bit. "Yes, I am," I smiled back at him.

"Don't be nervous, you will do wonderfully," he continued encouragingly and took off his brown horn glasses that he had previously put on to read his notes.

The nerves returned because I hadn't realised how obvious my inner turmoil was to outsiders. I really had to learn how to put on a poker face, especially if I wanted to work in the political field. "You really think so?" I asked hopefully, trusting that the question sounded genuine rather than childish.

"You have to stop doubting yourself. It's too time consuming and unnecessary. There is a reason why I invited you."

"All right," I agreed. "I really am looking forward to it, Marcello. Thank you for bringing me."

"You're welcome." He passed me a little booklet on the conference and his fingers lingered purposefully against my cold hand. An instant warmth pooled through me even after he withdrew his hand. "I think you will like the talk on poverty and innovation technology. We shall have a lot to discuss thereafter — after all, you are zealous about tackling poverty, while the talk concentrates on my field of expertise. Our conversations will be an interesting balance between passion and theory."

"You know, I have more to add than simply passion," I said, pleased about the confidence in my voice.

Though my attention was fixed on the little booklet, I could see Marcello study me through my peripheral vision. "Agreed. I am glad you see that too. I am getting a little tired of having to explain your potential to you."

I turned to face him. His eyes were full of sincerity. I wasn't used to seeing such intensity with his emotions except when we were in bed together. He was right. On paper, I was absolutely the accomplished young woman who could be seen with Marcello. Convincing myself of that fact was a different question. It was hard to commit to what I represented on paper.

"I am sorry," I said rather flatly.

"Don't be sorry. Just start believing in yourself. You'll do yourself a favour," he gave me another good look, placed his glasses back on his nose and returned his attention to his work. The rest of the journey remained in silence. Though he basically implied that I should take greater charge of my life, I still didn't have the courage to ask for a bathroom stop.

Eventually, we made it to the four-star hotel we were staying at. I tried to keep my expression as neutral as possible, firstly, because I wanted to appear professional if we were to run into any of Marcello's acquaintances and secondly, because I wanted to hide my amazement of the beautiful place we were going to spend the weekend at. Though I had spent time at fancy hotels for my parents' fifth anniversary or Mamma's fiftieth birthday, this conference was the first time I actually got to *stay* at the place. I had a feeling that I would feel like a complete fool. Just looking around the cars that were parked around us, silently shining in their glory, I knew that I was out of place.

Signor Lorenzo opened the car door for me and the July heat caressed my skin. The air had a hint of damp coolness, it must have been the ocean breeze. I straightened out my beige shorts and readjusted my blouse. In an utter hurry, I had bought both of these items with some cash I had found in my fake leather jacket after I had realised that I had very few items of clothing that would be appropriate for a conference.

Most of the clothes I had for university were too warm for the weekend and the rest of my wardrobe was either too short, too sexy or too old. When had I become such a shabby slut? It was not a conscious progression, I promise you. No wonder the male customers at Bianco knew how to tip well.

Marcello got out of the car and flung on his summer blazer. He met my eyes and smiled, which put me a little at ease. I made my way to the trunk, ready to grab my bag but Marcello gestured me to walk into the lobby with him. Though I didn't see him do it, I supposed Signor Lorenzo took care of that.

As Marcello and I entered the lobby, an uncomfortably cold shudder slithered down my damp back, and goosebumps appeared on my arms as if someone had pressed a button. My nerves were still concentrated in my stomach. An awful sensation. I had experienced the feeling when I first started going out with Silvio but those nerves had been a cause for excitement rather than dread.

Forcing myself not to walk behind him like an anxious little kid, I kept up with Marcello's quick strides and walked right next to him as we headed to the check-in desk. The lobby was so sophisticated, so elegant with porcelain vases in every corner and art deco furniture, I felt out of place immediately.

The crystal chandelier was so huge and majestic, I wondered whether the thing originated from a palace or whether it was a replica. The male employees behind the counters were so polished in their dark red suits and the female workers so put-together, I forced my gaze away from the apparent perfection and instead stared at a giant mirror with a Victorian gold frame. My shorts and shirt were creased while the sweat stains under my armpits were so much darker than I would have thought possible. I made an effort to let my arms dangle uselessly down my body, took another glance at my red face and directed my gaze to the floor. I really didn't look good.

While Marcello checked us in, a middle-aged couple walked to the desk right next to us. The man was lanky and quite handsome, especially in his light beige suit. He had the looks where you just knew he must have been quite a catch in his youth; the pronounced jawline, piercing blue eyes despite his raven black hair and his soft and enchanting chin dimple. But my stare preoccupied itself with the incredibly beautiful and tall woman who had her skinny arm loosely looped around the arm of the gentleman. Her softly curled hair was an unusual shade of blonde, the color of the first moments of the setting sun. The clothes were the definition of class; she wore a white summer suit, the fabric probably a luxurious linen, Louboutin heels and a wine-coloured Chanel bag. Heavy gold jewellery clung to her wrists and neck. This single outfit was probably worth double of everything that was hanging in my shabby closet in Monza. Her eyes were a crystallised yet cloudy shade of blue. Her heart-shaped face was of such striking symmetry even her eyebrows matched each other perfectly. She wore barely any make-up, her illuminating white skin radiant despite the soft wrinkles framing her eyes, the only indication of her age.

The breathtaking woman locked eyes with me. I must have been staring and felt my cheeks flush red, a wave of heat spreading through me despite the cold lobby. I turned away from her and looked down the marbled floor, trying to calm down. I truly had never felt so out of place.

"Marcello?" I heard a soothing female voice and realised it was the woman's. I looked at Marcello whose attention was pinned on the woman. The edges of his mouth tensed up. "I thought it was you," she added and smiled in a way which wasn't exactly unfriendly, but carried a hint of malice. Was this…? No, it couldn't be.

"Natala. Patrizio." Marcello extended his hand. I was so busy looking at the woman that I didn't realise that the lanky man had walked over to us and was now shaking Marcello's hand.

"You've made it. Wasn't the traffic awful?" asked the man, who must have been Patrizio.

"Yes, awful indeed," agreed Marcello, his look of neutrality returning.

The woman named Natala chuckled and said a little condescendingly, "It's not like Marcello did the driving himself, or have you got over yourself and actually sat behind the wheel?"

Ignoring the question, Marcello signed one of the

hotel forms, gave a short but clear nod of thank you to the employee behind the desk and readjusted his collar.

"Who is this?" asked Natala, and her eyes looked up and down my body. I might as well have been naked, I felt so exposed.

"Who-oh, yes." Marcello stumbled over his words, and I would have been offended by this glitch if I hadn't been so busy trying not to run out of the lobby. "This is Giovanna Ricci."

"Nice to meet you," she extended her hand, and I took it without hesitation. At least my polite reflexes hadn't given up on me. Her hand was soft, except for the part of her skin where two diamond rings pressed against my palm. Patrizio also extended his hand and nodded in acknowledgement. I still couldn't speak.

"So, what are you doing here, Giovanna?" asked Natala patronisingly.

I opened my mouth, completely oblivious to what words might be spoken when Marcello jumped in for me. "Giovanna just graduated top of her class from Bocconi's master's programme and is currently applying to jobs. She hopes to work in politics."

"Is that so?" asked Patrizio kindly and directed his gaze at me.

"Yes," I pressed out between my lips.

Marcello placed his arm behind my back and pushed me in the direction of the lift. "We'd better go and freshen up," he said to Patrizio and Natala.

"Oh yes, please don't let us hold you up,"

apologised Patrizio.

Marcello gave the couple a strained smile and told Patrizio that he would talk with him about some new acquisition later in the day. Then, Marcello and I walked away, his arm on my back pushing me a little forcefully towards the elevator. Stepping into the elevator, Marcello removed his hand from my back and waited for the doors to close. They shut behind us. He exhaled loudly.

We remained silent all the way to the hotel room. He pulled out the key card for the door but paused before he injected it into its slit. His eyes met mine, and he leaned down to give me a quick kiss. Taken aback, I didn't even really try to reciprocate the movement nor did I feel relaxed after the affectionate gesture. He was about to open the door when I placed my hand on his arm to stop him.

"Was that your ex-wife?" I asked steadily.

"Yes."

"Did you know she was coming?" My voice remained calm.

"I had a suspicion she would. Patrizio, her husband, is my business partner," he answered neutrally.

"You had a suspicion? It was a given." I said edgily.

Marcello nodded in response, and I had no idea what that meant. My insides were so angry, I didn't know how I managed to remain so collected. Why the hell didn't he tell me that his ex-wife was going to be here? I felt like such an idiot. I hated not knowing. And his ex-wife was so beautiful, the definition of the kind of woman Marcello should be with. But he was here with a girl who barely acted like a woman, who had no clue what she was doing with her life, was wearing cheap clothes and was in no way the kind of person an accomplished CEO should be with. I wanted to shake him, wanted to grab his blazer and rip it from him.

But I didn't. Instead, I nodded just like he did and removed my hand from his arm. He opened the door for us.

***

The talks in the afternoon had been intriguing, especially when the keynote speaker drew connections between Italy's financial crisis and the potential for selected businesses to collaborate in order to formulate innovative solutions. If I hadn't been so distracted with studying Natala who was sitting a couple of rows in front of us, it would have felt like I was back in the lecture hall listening to what my brilliant professors had to say. If the ex-wife of the man I was seeing hadn't been in this room, maybe I would have felt like I did belong at the conference, that I was good enough for these accomplished people.

After we had listened to several talks, Marcello and I walked from room to room though I kept a low profile. Whenever someone had recognised him, I excused myself to go and get some water or freshen up. He had never questioned my fabricated escapes though I could discern a look of puzzlement the fourth time I had come up with an excuse.

It wasn't even that I didn't visually fit into the scene even though I was one of the very few women around. I was wearing my one and only fitted pinstriped suit and wasn't that much younger compared to the other attendees. My red lipstick made me look older too, and in normal circumstances I would have said that I looked professional and quite sophisticated. But I was more concerned with the presence of Natala. This conference could have been my opportunity to find out whether I would fit in with these rich and accomplished people. And all I could think about was Marcello's ex-wife. I would never find out the details about what happened to the marriage, which wasn't that surprising given his lack of ability to talk about his childhood or his parents.

I saw a man appear out of a sea of dark suits. For the fifth time, I was about to excuse myself from Marcello, but he held my arm tightly and told me to stay. The blood pulsated in my ears.

"Signor Lombardi!" exclaimed the elderly man excitedly and shook Marcello's hand. "It is so nice to see you again. I am so glad to hear about your booming business. Congratulations, you have come a long way from when we last spoke."

"Thank you, Signor Giordano," Marcello replied politely.

My chest swelled in wonderful excitement as I recognised the man. It was *the* Ernesto Giordano. He was *the* leading politician trying to combat Italy's poverty. I had used so many of his writings in my thesis, I felt almost embarrassed to be standing in front of him. I just couldn't believe it was really him.

"May I introduce you to Giovanna Ricci?" asked Marcello conversationally. "She is a huge admirer of your work," he added and I was surprised that he had remembered. I had told him about my admiration for the statesman weeks ago.

The politician smiled, reached out his hand and I shook it with enthusiasm. I couldn't quite form the right words, yet I can assure you that I was smiling widely. "It is nice to meet you, Signora Ricci," he said and I gave him an even wider smile than I thought possible, not bothering to correct him of my marital status.

Finally, I found my voice again. "It is such an honour to meet you Signor Giordano, I cannot tell you how impressed I am by your efforts to battle the rise in Italy's poverty, especially with your new initiative you just introduced three weeks ago. I am so curious to see how your new framework will be implemented in practice," I spilled, pleasantly wondering where all these words came from.

"Thank you," he replied kindly. "I am glad to hear that the younger generation understands the pressing nature of the issue."

"Understand it?" I retorted excitedly. "I dedicated

my whole master's thesis to the topic. I compared the developmental policies of Italy and China."

"How wonderful, Signora Ricci!" he exclaimed with the same enthusiasm as he did when he saw Marcello. "What an intriguing combination. We need more young thinkers like you."

"Indeed," chimed in Marcello with a smile on his face. "The world needs to see more of Giovanna Ricci. She will go on to do great things, I am sure of it."

"No doubt there," agreed Signor Giordano. "It was wonderful to meet you, Signora Ricci, and lovely to see you again, Signor Lombardi. Unfortunately, I must return to a gentleman I might be collaborating with to implement the new framework, but I do hope we will all see each other again soon."

"Absolutely," I said when the politician extended his hand, which again, I shook with excitement. Then, Marcello said farewell and Signor Giordano disappeared as quickly into the sea of dark suits as he had appeared out of nowhere.

I beamed at Marcello. He squeezed my hand and whispered, "Perhaps you should stop running to the bathroom and actually circulate about the room to meet people." Though I was embarrassed that he saw right through my tactic, I couldn't help but chuckle at my own childishness. Perhaps I wasn't out of place after all. Perhaps I could be part of this society.

I had indeed met more of Marcello's successful acquaintances and experienced an academic buzz after meeting Ernesto Giordano. But the excitement had quickly transformed itself back into insecurity and dread. Not only did I see Natala dressed in a beautiful purple evening gown at the fancy conference dinner, which made my mother's black cheater dress look like sexy pyjamas, but I also couldn't help but feel intimidated and simultaneously jaded by the conversations at our table that evening. While the conversations with Silvio, Adamo and Elda were often devoid of any intellectualism, they were filled with jokes, cigarettes, laughter and aimless fun. Meanwhile, the financial crisis, some article in *The Economist* and the rising sea levels were all that these people here were capable of talking about. It was interesting, yes, but were these truly the only conversations that intellectual people could entertain themselves with? It appeared to be so.

Thankfully, the conference offered an abundance of alcohol, and I concentrated more on the wonderfully tasting gin cocktails than the conversations at our table. Marcello was in the midst of a lively talk on the newest tech innovation in the virtual reality field and didn't even notice how quiet I had become. Even the most considerate and conscientious of men could be so ignorant. But I had my gin buzz going, so I didn't really mind. I had to use the bathroom and was about to excuse myself from Marcello, but he was deep in conversation with some big shot engineer, so I just got up and walked through the beautiful dining room.

Once I arrived in the bathroom, it took a while for my vision to readjust because of the bright white lights that bathed the light grey marble in a coat of silver. Several scented candles were burning in the corner of the long row of sinks and emitted such a strong rose scent, it clouded my brain even further. I got into the cubicle and released my bladder from the great volume of alcohol. Pulling my underpants back up and straightening my dress, I walked out of the cubicle, washed my hands and gave myself a time out.

My reflection looked so tired, not from exhaustion, but from something else I couldn't quite pinpoint. There were dark rings under my eyes even though I had applied a good amount of concealer only a few hours ago. My dark lipstick looked dry and matt. Some of my mascara had flaked off, and I did my best to remove the little flakes with my fingers. The only thing that was still in place was my hair, which was slickly pulled back in a ponytail.

The tears came. They didn't run down my cheeks but quietly accumulated in my eyes. I placed my index finger on my cornea, allowing the liquid to slip onto my finger tip instead of ruining my base makeup, which was still in fairly good shape. I think I really missed Silvio. But before I could give my boyfriend any more thought, the last person I wanted to see walked into the bathroom.

"Oh, hello… Giovanna, was it?" Natala asked, and I hoped my eyes weren't ripped open too widely or my tears noticeable. I nodded and paused. Silence. Nothing could have prepared me for a one-on-one with Marcello's ex-wife.

"Well, have a great evening," I mumbled, tearing my attention away from her flawless face, and made my way to the bathroom exit but she blocked my path, forcing me to stop right in front of her. Her nude make-up was spotless. Not a single line was out of place.

"So, you are the girl Marcello is sleeping with?" she asked nonchalantly, although it was more of a statement than a question.

I could have given a hundred different responses. I could have told her it was none of her business, that I was not a girl but a woman, that the question was unjustified and should be directed towards her ex-husband, that I was proud to be with a man like Marcello. But all I said was, "Yes."

"Interesting," she added and started fiddling with her expensive and heavy gold chain that seemed to choke her skinny neck. "So, what do you want with him?"

"I'm sorry?" I asked, even though I heard her perfectly. I placed my hand against the marble sink, trying to find some sort of stability.

"I know he isn't incredible in bed," she started, and I tried my best to keep my expression neutral even though I could tell from the reflection of my peripheral vision that I looked petrified. "I mean he's not bad, but by the looks of you, you have had better, I'm sure of that. Oh, are you after his money? Or are you trying to sleep your way into the company? I can tell you right away that doesn't—"

"Signora," I began and broke off awkwardly because I had no idea what her last name was. "I don't know what happened between you and Marcello, he never told me. I am not after his money or any kind of job within his company. I have my reasons to be with him." I paused, allowing myself to take a breath. I was glad I'd had something to drink or otherwise I would have remained as mute as a statue. "So, please, I would like to return to the dining room."

Natala studied me for a minute with a mixture of stifled sadness and satisfaction. It made her look strangely old, and I only really realised then that she was about ten years older than Marcello. She finally moved away from the bathroom door. Pulling myself away from her perfect symmetry, I let go of the marble sink and made my way towards the bathroom exit. "No woman is ever going to be good enough for him," she said from behind me, which made me stop, though I didn't turn to face her. "And he's not capable of ever making a woman happy, I knew that from the moment I met him, and I am sure you do too."

Puzzled, I turned to look at her and was utterly unsettled by her expressionless face. I had no idea how to read her or what she was really trying to say.

"Then, why did you marry him?" I hated myself for sounding so childish.

She sighed, stemmed her arms against her hips in a defeated manner. "For the same reasons you are sleeping with him, Giovanna."

I went straight to the hotel room.

I didn't cry. I didn't freak out. I didn't drink the tiny bottles of overpriced vodka and rum that were stored in the room's mini fridge. I didn't reach for the three cigarettes I had packed for emergencies.

I just sat on the bed, my tired feet still touching the ground, and stared into space.

The scene in the bathroom seemed so surreal, so bizarre, I was trying to prove to my brain that it was a play of the many cocktails that I had. But I'd had way more to drink than that in the past, and I knew that talking to Natala was anything but a dream.

I threw off my ballet flats and laid down on the bed, not bothering to take my dress off, turn off the lights or get under the wonderfully soft sheets.

I fell asleep.

Though it felt like hours had passed, it was only half an hour later that Marcello woke me up, a look of concern framing his face. I looked at him, momentarily forgetting where we were and what had happened less than an hour ago. But then an overwhelming feeling of melancholy came over me and I turned away from him, trying to hide the tears that had crept their way back into my eyes.

"What happened, Giovanna?" he asked with such a note of concern in his voice, I felt like a twelve-year-old girl. This was the first time I truly wanted to slap him. I wanted to scream at him and tell him to mind his own business or to fucking talk to me about who the hell he really was.

"Your ex-wife," was all I choked and hated myself for truly playing the part of the kid. I reached for my cigarettes that I hid in the bedside drawer and lit one. It was a non-smoking room, but I really couldn't have cared less. I needed its comfort. I really did.

Marcello didn't protest or flinch even when I blew the smoke straight into his face. Instead, he placed his soft hand on my arm. I was angry at him, yet I couldn't help but feel instant comfort radiate from his hand. "You shouldn't ever listen to Natala. There is no point in listening to anything that she has to say."

And what I have to say is truly worth of anyone's time? I really wanted to ask, but instead went with the question I didn't think I had the nerve to ask, "Why did the two of you get divorced?"

He sighed, removed his hand from my arm and stared at the giant flat-screen TV that was across from the room. Then, he redirected his attention to me and replied, "My ex-wife looked great in photographs, she was the perfect accessory for public events," he began and for the first time since I had met him I could see a little bit of red spread into his cheeks despite the dim light. "But our conversations were flat and monotonous, probably a lot like you and Silvio." The mention of Silvio's name sliced into my heart, but Marcello didn't give me time to dwell on the guilt. I hadn't thought of Silvio in a couple of hours. That felt unnatural.

"Natala never even got close to the potential that you have," he continued, "She has never been capable of greatness and never will. *You* have what it takes, Giovanna. You have to learn to understand that."

I took another drag of the cigarette while Marcello dried my tears with his thumb. Gently, as if it were something delicate and fragile, he took the cigarette from between my fingers and extinguished it on the glass that was resting on the bedside. I felt oddly indifferent about him taking my comfort away from me. Then, he leaned down to kiss me.

Though I should have used the time to ask more about what Natala claimed and about what this man said, I just wanted to dive into a mindless state. I let Marcello kiss my neck as he undressed me. I let him take off my underpants and explore every inch of my body. And then I let him take me into the natural state of oblivion I wanted to escape into.

It was the best sex the two of us ever had.

When I woke up the next morning, Marcello was nowhere to be seen and not just because the curtains were drawn. Bewildered, I thought I had overslept and missed the last part of the conference but when I checked my phone, I realised it was seven. Then, I found a note on his pillow, which explained how he couldn't sleep and had gone to make some calls to Tokyo. I couldn't help but feel impressed and wondered whether I would ever be making calls to Japan. I liked that prospect.

The perfectly white soft sheets had the perfect mixture of calming coolness and warm softness, which made it hard to get out of bed. I pushed myself into an upright position and stretched my arms as wide as I could. With my feet, I pushed the blanket away from me and crawled out of bed. The muscles between my thighs burned with tension. I couldn't help but smile at last night's passionate moments, which now flashed in my head. It really was some amazing sex. The last time I had been sore because of that had probably been a year ago when Silvio and I had gotten so drunk that we couldn't remember when the sex started and ended.

I walked over to the window and opened the curtains. Brilliant sunlight pierced right into my eyes, and I squeezed them shut as fast as I could. After the initial surprise, I blinked a couple of times to let my vision readjust. I could make out the beauty of where I was. The hotel room was on top of one of Genoa's famous cliffs and looked down on the ocean. Patches of silver danced on the dark surface of the sea as the waves relaxed themselves into the hands of the playful winds. As I observed the spectacle, I wondered whether I saw a tiny little fisher boat within the glitter, but it was hard to tell within the jumble of light. Nature at its finest tranquillity. Simply magnificent.

Before I knew it, I felt tears leak out of my eyes, which rolled down my cheek and gently caressed my skin as they made their way to my chin. The sadness was so overwhelming, I wrapped my arms around myself to try and find some sort of comfort in the personal embrace, yet it only reminded me of how lonely I felt.

I looked away from the beautiful morning and drew my attention to my phone, which was clutched in my hand. Without conscious thought, I dialled Papà's number.

"Giogio?" I heard his comforting voice crackle through the phone and felt relieved that he had picked up.

"Papà," I tried to contain a sob but not very successfully.

"Are you all right?" he panicked. "Are you hurt?"

I swallowed hard and paused to give myself some time to think of the best way of telling my father the biggest secret I ever had. "I'm fine Papà, it's nothing like that."

"Where is Silvio?" he asked a little more calmly.

"He is… not here. I'm… in Genoa."

"Geno—?" he cut off his exclaim to readjust his voice to a more neutral register though I could tell that he had trouble with that. "Giovanna, what on earth is going on?"

"I'm at a conference," I opened the window and the warm ocean wind tickled my face encouragingly. It was time. "I am here with another man, Papà."

As expected, there was silence. Papà wasn't the sort

of man to shout and scream. Calmness and a collected mindset was what he always tried to teach me when I would act out as a teenager. It certainly was a valuable approach though I sort of wished that Papà would lose his composure for the biggest bomb I ever had in store.

"Who is this man?" he asked.

"A CEO of an innovation technology start-up, in his mid-thirties." For some reason I thought it was important to get all the facts out. "He went to Bocconi and *The Economist* recently did a profile on him."

"That's fine," his collected voice didn't have a hint of emotion. "But what sort of man is he?"

"A very successful one."

"Yes, Giovanna, but I'm really asking about his personality. Does he treat you right? There must be a reason why you are with him."

"He treats me right," I nodded, even though Papà obviously couldn't see that. "I think I'm with him because I feel like I'm getting closer to the version of myself that I'm supposed to be."

"And what version is that?"

"The one that takes Silvio out of the equation." My tears had finally dried. I felt a burning thirst scratch the back of my throat.

"I gather Silvio doesn't know about the affair?" he asked steadily.

"No. And I don't want him to find out." I took a breath and leaned my head against the window frame, which had become quite warm in the morning sun. "I think… I think I made a mistake with this man. I don't know if I can be this academic, intellectual and glamourous version that I would have to be to fit in."

"Why don't you stop worrying about the sort of version you are forcing yourself to be and think about what is important to you." His composure began to fade a little and a subtle hint of impatience pressed its way into my ear. "You are no longer a child, Giovanna, stop worrying about who you should and shouldn't be and just *be.*"

That is exactly what I don't know how to do, I wanted to tell him but didn't. Papà was already disappointed in me, I didn't want to admit how much trouble I had with simply existing and accepting myself. I let my arm dangle loosely out of the window and the ocean breeze tickled my skin comfortably. The hand clutching the phone was starting to go limp as I was squeezing the object so hard.

"You have to choose." Though Papà was forceful about the statement, the pointed tone was full with fatherly affection. "Between Silvio and this new man. No good can come from having both in your life."

"Can you help me choose, Papà?" I asked, this time not caring that I truly did sound like a child. When it came to family, I think that was all right.

"No, I can't, Giogio," he answered patiently. "All you have to ask yourself is who makes you happy and can give you what you expect from the man in your life."

The warmth of the sun began to settle on my skin, and I could feel a subtle sweat emerge from below my armpits. I took another look at the playful silver patches illuminating the ocean in hypnotising brilliance and moved away from the window to walk back into the cool shade of the luxurious hotel room. It wasn't until I placed myself on the bed that I spoke again, "I don't know if either of them can seriously give me what I expect and need."

"Well, what do you want from a man?"

"Love." The answer escaped my mouth, before I could even formulate the word in my head. I was quite surprised by my subconscious answer. I didn't really know that was what I really wanted… because Silvio gave me exactly that.

"Does this other man give you love?" Papà asked, and I started to get a little irritated. I felt like I was at a doctor's office or in therapy.

"Not in the way that Silvio does." I paused and crawled back under the wonderfully soft bedsheets. "So, it must be Silvio then."

"It doesn't have to be anyone, Giovanna. I also know that you can be independent, without a man, and still be happy. You are strong enough."

Happiness without a man? Even before Silvio, I had always defined myself by the man I had a crush on or I had been with. Honestly, the last time I had been without a boy in my life was when I was fourteen. That was over a decade ago. I couldn't possibly find happiness without having a man in my life, I had no idea where to start. That wasn't all that surprising; I only ever had male figures to guide me, so I never learned how to be an independent woman. The person who was supposed to teach me that had abandoned her child and left for New York. I really, really didn't want to be alone. And having a man in my life had always been the way that I ensured not to walk down a solitary road.

So far, Papà had always been spot on when it came to my capabilities and emotions. He had always determined the next steps I would take, always had a sense of what grades I would get, when I would move out to live with Silvio or what master's degree I would pursue. Papà really knew me better than I did myself, so if he said I could do it all on my own, I am sure he wasn't wrong. Maybe I could make it without a man. But I just didn't want to.

***

I never thought I would feel so lost and discomforted when I left Monza behind. Leaving home apparently meant that I had departed from the version of Giovanna that I had become so accustomed to. Genoa had transformed me into a professional and put-together person I didn't know I could be, even though it was a superficial façade. And I didn't know if I wanted to submit to the role fully. In many ways, I thought this was the person I could and had to be given my education. I finally understood what Marcello had always talked about when he kept telling me that I was the embodiment of unfulfilled potential. The feeling of accomplishment and desire for more had bloomed in my thoughts almost immediately after Ernesto Giordano had been impressed by *my* master's thesis. Apparently, the months I had spent writing the 'thing' — as Silvio liked to call it — mattered a tiny bit, if only for a conversation starter with an incredibly accomplished politician.

And yet I had felt unsettled the whole time. I hadn't been able to compartmentalise between the opportunities of the conference and the presence of Marcello's ex-wife. The capacity of putting your personal life to the side seemed to be an important step to becoming a ruthless career woman, but I had a feeling that I might not be capable of doing that. Perhaps I represented more potential than Natala. I wanted to believe Marcello. But having more to give to the world than his ex-wife didn't seem worth very much if all I craved was security and a predictable future, which Silvio could offer me. And most importantly, even though Marcello had been right next to me most of the time, I had felt so incredibly lonely. I hadn't noticed it before but this weekend had made me realise that whenever I was with Marcello, I was alienated from him, even when our bodies fused into one. We had a connection, yet that really didn't matter if he made me feel more alone and anxious than when I wasn't with him.

Through a miracle, Marcello and I had not run into Natala on the last day of the conference even though we had gone to two more talks. I hadn't paid real attention to them. All I had thought about this morning was my true love. Silvio. I wanted Silvio and wanted to forget everything about this bizarre weekend. It was the first time I truly wished Marcello had never walked into Bianco on the day it had all started.

Signor Lorenzo took care of our luggage, while Marcello opened the car door for me with a smile. All I could manage was a small twitch of my lips and got into the car, the leather squeaking when I slid in. Though I am sure that Marcello had noticed that I was a lot quieter than usual all morning, he let me be. I was grateful for that.

A few minutes into the car ride, Marcello spoke, "Did you enjoy the conference?"

"I did," I lied steadily and pulled *The Economist* out from my bag. This time it was me who really didn't want to talk. I hoped he would get the hint.

"What was your favourite part?"

"Hmm, let me think," I began quite sarcastically and I felt instant frustration pierce from the pit of my stomach and into my voice. "How about the part where I met your ex-wife? Or the part where I had a little one-on-one talk with her? Truly inspiring conversations, I must say."

"Giovanna, I thought we were done with this." I

could see him glance a little uncomfortably at Signor Lorenzo. I couldn't help but feel satisfied; it was good to know that I definitely had the ability to make him feel unsettled too. It was a two-way street after all. "You would have never met Ernesto Giordano, if you hadn't come with me."

"And I would have never met your ex-wife if I hadn't," I shot back reproachfully. Our eyes met, and I found something in his gaze that I hadn't seen before. Hurt? Guilt? Both? Interesting. I didn't know what to make of that, so I paused, and we continued to look at each other while the blue sky and grey trees framing the highway whizzed outside his window. Marcello had such beautiful blue eyes. They still had the ability to comfort me.

"I'm sorry," I began after I steadied my emotions. "It really was a good conference. I appreciate that you wanted to share it with me." And I truly felt that way.

"I am glad," his expression softened. "Would you like to come home with me?"

Suddenly, Signor Lorenzo inhaled sharply. The car made a rough jolt, my insides jumped inside my body as if someone had thrown them into the air. I pressed my arms against the driver's seat to soften the blow of the abrupt halt, but I couldn't help but bang my head against the window. Instant pain swelled where the glass collided with the left side of my head.

Then I blinked and was surprised to see the car driving reassuringly its regular highway speed, as if nothing had happened.

"I am so sorry, Signor Lombardi, Signorina Ricci," exclaimed Signor Lorenzo while I pushed myself back into my seat, rubbing my aching head. "The car in front of me just came to an abrupt halt, I had to hit the brakes this hard," he continued anxiously while he concentrated on the street, his shoulders and arms still tense form the physical shock.

"That's fine," replied Marcello reassuringly. "It's Italian traffic, it happens." He returned his attention to me. "You all right, Giovanna?"

"Yes, yes, just a little bump on the head but nothing to worry about," I replied and withdrew my hand from the source of the pain, which was subsiding quite quickly. The pain had more to do with the sudden surprise than the actual impact.

"You're sure?" he was genuinely concerned.

"Absolutely," I told him reassuringly, "and you can drop me off at the train station. I would like to go home and rest."

"If you like," he nodded. He pulled out his laptop from his briefcase, placed his glasses on his nose and turned his attention to work. The rest of the car ride into Milano was just as silent as most of the way when we departed for Genoa.

As soon as he had dropped me off at the train station and driven out of sight, I bought a pack of Marlboros and indulged in three cigarettes.

Finally, I was on my way back to Monza. The

shapes that swooshed past the windows of the train leading out of Milano were moving too quickly for my overly crammed brain to identify any distinctive colours or architecture. The buildings blended into one strange shade of grey with a hint of pale green. It was about to rain, perhaps that was the cause of the sickly shades that painted the metropolitan city.

I leaned my head against the satisfyingly cold window and closed my eyes. My mind couldn't process the haziness of the rapidly moving city any more. My body felt so heavy, even my bony fingers didn't seem to want to move, so I let them rest loosely on my legs. I felt goosebumps creep onto my skin and longed for the cardigan I had tied around my bag. But my arms dangled numbly down my body as if they were not my own. I would have to let the cold feed its way under my skin.

Monza was home. Monza was where Silvio and Papà had more love to spend on me than the whole city ever could. I just told my father that I was cheating on a man, and he showered me with advice and care, not a hint of condescending opinions. He just needed me to be happy. The Milanese politicians and business men were the leaders, but were they capable of an affection that represented the unrestricted love that Monza embodied for me?

Unconditional love had been my sole source of true happiness; there was only so much superficial satisfaction that cigarettes, alcohol and the occasional vacation to Rimini could bring. I could see the potential of how new sources could collectively shape a form of happiness, but would that measure up to what I had known? Wasn't the linearity of having one person love you a lot more efficient?

***

A week had passed since the conference. I hadn't texted, called or seen Marcello for the past seven days. Instead, I had enjoyed the sanctity of Monza. Somehow, despite his excellent skill of predicting people's behaviour, Silvio hadn't seen through my lie of spending the weekend at Papà's. Perhaps our strained relationship distracted him from sensing that I was a cheater behind the curtains. But I was incredibly grateful for his unawareness; my boyfriend was the man I should be with, I just needed that to be true. Being with him made life so much easier.

On the last day of July, Marcello called and asked me to come over.

It was time to break it off.

I walked into his brilliantly white apartment, which I planned would be the last time. When Marcello saw me walk into the living room, he took off his glasses, placed the laptop he was working with on the glass table and walked over to me. He hesitated, then gave me a soft kiss on the lips. He pulled away, placed his hand on my cheek and leaned down to give me another, more passionate kiss even though he must have tasted the smoke staining my mouth. I couldn't help it, I lost myself in his mouth, in his touch, in his soft body. Marcello had me under some sort of unexplainable trance, which pulled me back to him. The attraction I felt apparently hadn't diminished in the slightest despite the discomfort the conference caused.

But the humiliation of the memory still made me want to push Marcello away. I couldn't give in now. I had come here with a purpose. "Can you get me a bottle of Cabernet Sauvignon from your wine cellar?" I asked, fully conscious that he would not be pleased about this question, which might make the ending of us easier.

He nodded, walked into the kitchen and brought me a glass. Then, he walked towards the corridor where the wine cellar was hiding behind the bookshelf and returned to me with a bottle of luxury. I'd never heard of the wine, so I was sure it was expensive. "I bought it for you." He poured me a glass, passed it to me and placed the bottle on the glass table. It was odd that he told me that the bottle was intended for me because it wasn't like he was going to drink it. For a second I thought whether he had had another affair but quickly dismissed the thought; Marcello was such a busy man and barely had time to spend with me, there was no way he could squeeze in another woman between his work.

I took a sip of the wonderfully bitter and sweet wine and gestured for us to sit down on the couch. The leather of the couch squeaked as we settled ourselves onto its modern comfort. I took another sip of wine and carefully placed it on the coaster that was lying solitarily on the glass table.

It was time.

"We have to stop seeing each other," I said calmly and was surprised by how easily these words came from my mouth. Perhaps it helped knowing that I was finally ending things, so it didn't matter whether I took a wrong step now. And anyway, Marcello had probably lost a lot of respect for me after the conference. His expectations were just too high.

The man looked at me expressionlessly and simply blinked.

"I am not the woman you need me to be," I continued just as calmly as before, "We have to end this."

"You sound like Natala, not like yourself," he said, still without emotion. "She talks a lot of shit and it's always untrue, so can we just move on now? I promise you, she is no threat whatsoever. Giovanna, I want you in my life. We are good together. Whether you see it, is up to you."

I was stunned. Not only did Marcello swear, which was a first, but I had also never heard him speak such a long strand of sentences except when he spoke of work. Amazing. There were so many things I hadn't discovered about this man. I was curious to learn more.

No. *Stop it, Giovanna.*

"Marcello, I need this to stop." I grabbed my glass

and took two big gulps, the liquid burning a little in the back of my throat.

"At least let me help you with your future."

"I can't choose between sleeping with you and you mentoring me," another gulp of wine. The glass was already empty. "Those things have blended into one."

"I think you should think about going to New York," he said as he poured me another glass. "Your mother is there, so you won't be alone."

Though I knew I should have redirected my words to ending things, I asked, "Don't you want me here?" I couldn't expel the note of hurt in my voice nor my confusion; I didn't understand why he would bring up Mamma, it was quite rude. He knew she was a sore subject and had been respectful of that so far. I knew Marcello did it now to throw me off course, he knew how to play dirty.

"Of course, I do, I just think you would find it educational and exciting."

I started to get irritated then, took the glass from Marcello and gulped down the wine as if it were water. It seemed like the appropriate thing to do. "Are you listening to me? I don't want your help. I can do this without you."

There it was, the twitching of the lips, the gesture that irritated me the most. I wasn't a little girl any more. "Narcissism can blossom or stunt potential," he began. "Which way it goes is up to the person."

He might as well have slapped me. Had I really

turned into such a narcissist? But how was that possible? I was here to break it off with Marcello because I *didn't* think I was good enough for him. I knew I was not accomplished enough for him. I knew I wasn't composed enough, not beautiful enough, not intellectual enough. And here he was suggesting I was a narcissist. Who the hell did he think he was? *He* was the narcissist.

I emptied my wine glass, got up from the couch and walked towards the corridor that led to the exit of his apartment. I wanted to do things the adult way and have a pragmatic conversation, but Marcello knew how to throw me off the tracks. I didn't have the patience to stay composed. Walking out on him seemed like the only option.

Of course, Marcello took my new course of strategy from me when he grabbed my arm from behind and twirled me, so we were face to face. The harsh corridor light bathed us in white, we looked like two entangled ghosts. Our foreheads almost touched. His clean breath intoxicated my nostrils. The grip on my arm was pleasurably painful as he forced his lips on mine. He was desperate. Another first. Though I resisted him initially, I was so attracted to his determination and charge, submitting to him felt like the natural course of action.

I didn't want to leave. I couldn't leave.

So, I didn't.

After the First Weekend of August

I folded my clothes. I tried placing them neatly in my suitcase, which proved difficult because of the curtain of tears that blurred every colour and every edge into one pattern of confusion. The T-shirt I was holding slipped through my fingers, and as I crouched down to pick it up, my feet just gave away. With a loud thump, I collapsed on the floor and rested my hands against my cheeks. My cheeks were so wet, I might as well have gotten out of the shower. The pain of my broken heart almost felt physical. Sometimes, my body heaved as it tried to gasp for breath. I cried harder than when Mamma had left for New York. I had heard phone calls all morning. I ignored them. It was either Papà asking whether I needed help packing or possibly Marcello. For once in my life, I just wanted to be alone for a few hours.

The moment I had rejected Silvio's proposal, I could not only hear his and my heart shatter at my response but I could see my future of security dissolve into invisible particles of air, as if that possibility had never been there.

The affair was no longer an affair. It could have been a relationship. But my heart was broken and I knew that Marcello would never be the one to mend it. Though I had never told him in person — he would have convinced me to stay — I had texted that it was over. Not very adult-like but I really couldn't have cared less. He had tried calling a few times, but I ignored him. So over. It should have been right after the conference, I just hadn't had the willpower to break it off with Marcello because of his charm and the abundance of wine, even though I knew that I never felt lonelier than when I was physically there with him.

Oh, Silvio. How much I loved you. But as soon as I saw you present me with that beautiful ring, everything was so crystal-clear. I couldn't settle for unconditional love and security. I didn't work this hard just to be a domestic house wife, which was the woman you really needed to be with. Only she could get close to reciprocating the love that you had to offer. And that person was never supposed to be me. I am so sorry, Silvio. I am so, so sorry.

Because my vision was obstructed by a colourless curtain, my hand searched the wooden floor for the T-shirt I had just dropped. When I found its softness crease between my fingers, I formed a fist around the dark and blurry cloth. I blinked and realised that the piece of clothing wasn't mine. It was Silvio's black Daft Punk shirt that he slept in. Slightly choking, I pressed it against my face, breathing deeply to take in his scent through the snot and tears that had overtaken all my senses. But Silvio's scent was so sweet, strong and familiar that it was easy for me to discern as much of him as possible. His scent alone gave me so much pleasure and comfort, it was quite ridiculous.

I heard the door to the apartment unlock and quickly got on my feet. Silvio had texted he would be working all day so I could go and collect my things, but maybe he had forgotten something. Or maybe he was so angry that he just wanted to slap me, which would be more than justified.

"Don't you ever pick up your phone?" I heard a hectic voice shout and it took me a second to realise that it was Adamo's. When he found me, he was panting with an expression of anger and nervousness engraved on his face.

"Adamo?" I asked in surprise, my sobs and tears stopping immediately as if they were only part of my imagination.

"Giovanna, what the hell? You've got to pick up your phone! It's Silvio!"

My heart sank so deep into the pit of my stomach, I was shocked it didn't fall straight out of my body.

"Is he hurt?" I walked towards Adamo, grabbed him by his arms and started shaking him. "What happened? Please tell me he's OK!"

Adamo paused and laid his hands on my shoulder. The weight was comforting although my thoughts were bouncing uncontrollably inside my brain. "Silvio is OK," he said quite calmly. "He isn't hurt. But I think he might hurt the man you have been sleeping with."

I let go of Adamo's arms immediately. He still held onto mine. It felt like someone grabbed my lungs and ripped them out of my body in one rapid movement. For a couple of seconds, I couldn't breathe. I must have felt immense pain in my chest though I couldn't discern anything.

"When...? How...?" My voice started working again though oxygen still hadn't entered my body. "What?"

Adamo squeezed my shoulders, clearly grappling between trying to hurt me for what I had done to his best friend and getting the facts out in a constructive fashion. "He told me last night about this Lombardi. Silvio found some conference booklet when you were unpacking, checked it out online and found dozens of photos of you in a suit, always standing next to the same man." He said all this almost conversationally but then added reproachfully, "If he hadn't placed his hand on your back in every single one of them, then maybe you would have got away with it."

If possible, the million pieces of my already shattered heart broke into even smaller ones. Silvio had known. I wanted to ask how he reached the conclusion that I was sleeping with the man in the photographs, but it didn't matter. It was too late, and Silvio wasn't wrong. Guilt became a word devoid of meaning.

"Why did Silvio propose to me?" I whispered.

Adamo loosened his strong grip on my shoulders and let go of me, a sad expression vacant of any anger framed his face.

"Because he didn't want to lose the woman he loved," he said.

The tears that had run dry as soon as Adamo walked into the apartment had found their way into my eyes again. The face of my friend turned into a wobbly blob of beige and black, which was a good thing, because it meant I didn't have to look at his disappointment.

Adamo needed a breather, so we took a moment for the information to sink in. Then, he continued, "He is looking for him, Giovanna. I don't know where Silvio is but I know that he left the car dealership without a word after he figured out where the man is."

I wanted to tell Adamo that I was no longer having the affair, that I broke it off in the moment I ruined Silvio's heart. But right now, I had to find Silvio. "What is he trying to do?" I choked though genuinely curious. Silvio was a strong man who could cause damage, no question, but it really wasn't in his nature to do harm to others.

"I don't know, Giovanna, I really don't. He left his phone at work."

I nodded, grabbed my purse and walked past Adamo but stopped. "I am so sorry Adamo," I began, "I never wanted for him to get hurt."

Not turning around, Adamo sighed and said, unbearably defeated, "This was the last thing I did for you, Giovanna. From now on, you're on your own."

I looked at the silhouette of my friend. I wiped

away the tears that were pooling out of my eyes because of the loss of a loyal friendship. Then, I left the apartment and Adamo behind.

***

As I ran through the financial district of Milano, I ignored the August heat that stuck to every inch of my body. There was no time to complain to myself about the Italian summer weather. My lungs were burning and phlegm accumulated in the back of my throat. Smoking really was so bad for you. But my mission to find Silvio was much stronger than the pain that was reverberating through my body.

Knowing Marcello, the most plausible place he would be on a Wednesday morning was in his office. I had never been there, but I knew exactly where I had to go. The trip felt like the longest journey I ever had to undertake, but eventually the blue-grey skyscraper stood in front of me. I didn't have time to feel intimidated by the enormous building or the sea of suits that were speed-walking in and out of the building. My shabby orange dress was a lot more dishevelled compared to the other time I had been wearing it to seek refuge in Marcello's apartment. I really had to throw this dress out; not only was it old, but clearly it was tainted with disaster.

Running towards the entry of the building, I wanted to give myself a few seconds rest to catch my breath.

The moment I stopped running, the unbearable pain expanding in my lungs, legs and heat clung onto me. I couldn't repress a gasp of pain. My brain commanded my body to keep going, pushing the bodily complaints to the side. Several men stared in confusion as a blur of orange rushed past them into the building, but there was no time to care. Ignoring the welcome desk, I ran straight to the elevators and felt an instant relief once I was engulfed in an icy cloud of air-conditioning. I hit the button, and one of the twelve elevators opened right away. I lunged into emptiness and pressed the button that made the doors shut immediately even though it felt like they were moving in slow motion.

My hand wanted to press the button for Marcello's floor but they were all without a label. A cry of frustration formed in the back of my throat. There were twenty floors of this giant building, trying to find the right one via trial and error would take ages. Thankfully, I located the directory on the other side of the elevator and found one description as *Lombardi & Company: Innovation Technology*, which could be found on the sixteenth floor. I pressed the right button and the elevator finally hummed its way up to Marcello's floor.

Sprinting out of the elevator into an empty and glossy white lobby, I turned the corner, hoping to find any sign of life. I ran down a long corridor, and then got rooted to the spot as if I ran into a glass wall I didn't see before.

Silvio stood in the middle of the office while hard-working employees were plastered to their desks. He was still wearing his mechanic uniform and faced away from me. I tried to take a step towards my ex-boyfriend to announce my presence but my legs wouldn't move. Then, a beautiful woman who must have been a secretary walked towards Silvio and to my dismay Marcello followed right behind her. The office was completely oblivious to the fact that two men who had slept with the same woman were facing each other for the very first time.

"Signor Marino has been asking for you," said the secretary to Marcello in a singsong sort of voice. "I will leave you two gentlemen to it." She disappeared behind a desk.

"How can I help you, Signor Marino?" asked Marcello but there was a lack of curiosity or sincerity in the question. Something told me that he knew who Silvio was as soon as he saw him standing in his office, despite not showing any indication of recognition. Silvio seemed incapable of saying anything, so Marcello asked, "You must be here for my car, thank you for accommodating me on such short notice. Shall we go into the garage and I'll show you the issue?" Marcello gestured towards the elevators and saw me stand in his office. Though he couldn't hide his immediate surprise, his face returned to his usual composure, and he redirected his attention to Silvio who was still watching the man who had slept with his woman.

Silvio found his voice. "No… no, actually I think—" he broke off and whispered something I couldn't hear though I could see him take a deep breath.

"Of course, I understand," Marcello nodded neutrally. "Naturally taking totalled cars off the road takes priority."

"I will send someone as soon as possible, I am sorry for the inconvenience," I heard him say a little more confidently now.

"No worries," Marcello assured him. "I wish you a good day." Silvio nodded but didn't move a muscle to initiate a departure. Marcello looked over my ex-boyfriend's shoulder and locked his eyes with mine. I tilted my head a little bit to the side and opened my mouth to allow fresh air to fill my lungs. Then, I shook my head with as little movement as possible, for no reason in particular. I just felt the need to communicate something to Marcello, it wasn't his place to say anything.

"So, you are *the* Marcello Lombardi?" Silvio voiced the thought, although it was more of a statement than a genuine question.

"Yes, indeed, I am the founder of this company." Marcello gestured his arm to the side where the workers were still oblivious to this conversation.

"No, I mean," Silvio hesitated, clenched his fists and then said steadily, "You have completely altered the course of my life, haven't you?"

"I don't know about that," Marcello didn't miss a

beat, "but I am flattered that the innovations we develop here have such a great impact."

"A great impact," Silvio chuckled in quiet disbelief and his fists clenched even tighter. "Indeed, you cannot deny that."

"Now, I really must return a phone call, Signor Marino," continued Marcello and took a step backwards, "It was a pleasure to meet you."

Silvio didn't answer and gave a firm nod instead. He took another look at the man who had slept with the woman he was in love with. Then he turned and headed for the exit.

It wasn't until I saw Silvio's look of bewilderment and weird amazement that I remembered that I was standing right there in the office. The scene felt so surreal, so distant, almost as if I had been watching the two men interact in a terrible show on TV. But it was all too real. My ex-boyfriend's surprise turned into an unreadable expression I had never encountered before. After a six-year relationship, I didn't think that was possible. He walked towards me. The closer he got, the more I felt my tears press their way onto my skin, though I did my best to hold them back. A glassy haze obstructed my vision. I blinked, two simultaneous tears dripped down my cheeks.

Silvio stood in front of me, barely a foot away. Our eyes locked, so much love, all our years of good and troubled times suspended between the two of us. I took a deep breath and so did he. He tore his gaze from mine and looked me up and down as if he saw me for the first time. Then, our eyes locked once again for the very last time.

And without a word, Silvio walked out of my life.

In that moment I couldn't move, the shock and sadness consumed all my energy, movement seemed like an irrational action. My focus was still plastered to where Silvio's face had been. Tears were abundantly flooding like a little well that only knew how to channel water into a stream. I listened to the footsteps of my first true love fade. All I heard now was the busy typing and scribbles of the employees that were oblivious to the potential drama that could have unfolded right in this office.

I was still staring at the spot where Silvio had stood and readjusted my vision to find Marcello looking at me impassively. He didn't walk towards me, and he didn't walk away. He didn't look angry to see me, and he didn't look pleased. This time was different, this time he allowed me to make the choice to walk away. I looked at the man I had admired and who had let me believe I could be the accomplished woman he wanted me to be. I took in the comforting softness around Marcello's enchanting blue eyes, which gave me the strength to revitalise. My breathing returned to a regular rhythmic fashion. The feeling in my legs and arms returned. It was time for me to leave the other man behind.

Emotionless, I let my lungs fill with the cool air of the office, tore my gaze away from the man and slowly walked away from the things that could have been.

Epilogue

The First Day of September

The change of the month brought a subtle coolness in the air as if the weather knew the summer days were coming to an end. Wearing my fitted pin-striped suit wasn't as terrible as I thought it was going to be. I was still hot but that had more to do with nerves rather than the weather. A pleasant excitement tingled in the tips of my fingers, and I couldn't help but smile to myself. Embracing the incalculable future was daunting but also promised unforeseeable thrills.

I was sitting on the train to Milano. I usually studied the impressive architecture and busy streets on my way into the city, but this time I dedicated the ride to my notes resting on my lap.

The interview had to go well. It was the perfect job for me: a junior political analyst for a regional constitution outside of Rome. My potential employer had a recruitment office here in Milano, and they really liked my resumé that I had sent in two weeks before.

Expecting a job to fall into your lap was a symptom of vanity and laziness. Papà had been right, it really did take over twenty applications to get an interview with an employer who was willing to pay. Knowing that I was incredibly nervous about the job interview, Papà had been so sweet and had not only prepared me breakfast in bed but also bought me a bouquet of lilies to wish me good luck. It felt so good living with him again. The thought that I might have to move out soon if I were to get the job was quite upsetting. But promising.

It's been three weeks since Silvio stood in Marcello's office. I hadn't seen either of them since then and wasn't planning on it. I didn't know for sure what Marcello was doing, I had a strong feeling that he had just returned to what he was good at — work and bringing success to his company. Meanwhile, I knew that Silvio was doing as well as a man could who found out that his girlfriend was cheating on him and got rejected when proposing with a ring that was impossible to say no to. I would be lying if the thought of calling him, apologising and declaring my love for him hadn't occurred to me. Of course, it had. I had even made my way to what used to be our apartment; I had just wanted to feel his strong arms around me, his comforting scent mingle with mine. But I had restrained myself.

Though Adamo didn't speak to me any more, Elda told me that Silvio was doing all right and was training extremely hard for the upcoming marathon. But she had refused to tell me more when I asked for details. I suppose that was fair. Still, I had cried and begged her to tell me more, just like a little girl would have. When it came to Silvio, I was still acting irrationally. I loved him. The strength of that emotion would fade with time but never extinguish.

I had been stuck between Monza and Milano for twenty-five years. And I shattered everything that I had built. I was the architect of a city and simultaneously the hurricane that destroyed the years of careful construction. It was painful to know that I would never sit outside with Silvio, Elda and Adamo and drink, smoke and laugh about anything and everything. On the other hand, I didn't think I would be sitting on the train right now, trying to chase a new life; the rupture triggered an opportunity, and it was my duty to pursue these new chances that I created through the turbulence and my education.

Without any sort of validation from a man, I was blossoming into a natural version of myself. An overdue course of action, but it's never too late to loosen the forceful grip of control. Things were changing, and it finally felt like life was falling into place.

The notes on my lap rustled quietly in unison with the comforting vibration of the train. The excitement tingled in my fingertips as I flicked through the pages. I glanced out of the window and realised the train was following different tracks; the buildings that I had gotten to know so well were no longer paving the way.